THE DEATH COLLECTOR

A VICTORIAN MURDER MYSTERY FROM
TONI MOUNT

The
Death Collector

A Victorian Murder Mystery

M
MadeGlobal Publishing

For more information on
MadeGlobal Publishing, visit
our website
www.madeglobal.com

Cover butterfly image: Anthony
Hillman, Copyright 2018 ©
MadeGlobal Publishing

With thanks to the Gravesend Library
Creative Writing Group for their friendship,
enthusiasm and encouragement and for
whom I finally finished this story.

People begin to see that something more goes to the composition of a fine murder than two blockheads... a knife, a purse and a dark lane...

'On Murder Considered as One of the Fine Arts'
Thomas de Quincey, 1827

PROLOGUE

I AM a collector. As a small boy, I collected butterflies and beetles, pinning them carefully onto display boards.

'Nathaniel,' Nanny would say, 'I am certain you are supposed to kill them kindly, first. Not leave them to flutter and wave their legs until they die of exhaustion.'

But I would watch them, timing their death throes and noting them down in my book. Not that she knew that; she thought I was recording the species and where I had found them, as other collectors of such things do.

However, insects became a dull subject for my studies – they gave in to death so silently. My brother Nigel's pet rabbit screamed when it died; I made certain of that as I broke each of its legs in turn before I 'hanged it by the neck until dead', as they say. The local community of cats and dogs began to disappear, even my mother's parrot – hateful, squawking thing – and a sheep, on one occasion. At first, I wondered whether I had the strength and courage necessitated by the dispatch of larger beasts but, once having experienced the proportionally greater thrill and satisfaction, I was determined. After due consideration, for a brief while, until I grew bored by the lack of novelty, a slit throat became my chosen method. I was surprised and delighted by the copious amounts of blood but the disposal of my gore-grimed clothing, along with a convincing story for Nanny to explain the loss of attire, proved irksome and tedious, if instructive for my later career.

I taught myself how to dissect the bodies, learning the purpose and position of each organ. I studied the anatomy of every specimen, examining muscles, tendons, nerves and blood vessels in detail. In the early days, a magnifying glass sufficed but, for my thirteenth birthday, I requested and received a compound microscope that enhanced my work considerably.

The difficulty was that such large corpses could not be kept for display purposes, so my collection took on a literary form of detailed notes and drawings. As a fine draughtsman, the latter became the main element of my studies until I acquired the advantage of photography with the purchase of a camera in 1871. 'Le Phoebus' was an intriguing instrument built of mahogany wood with a brass mounted lens and the possibility of adjusting the focus to project a sharp image onto a ground glass plate at the back. As I became proficient in its use, able to judge to perfection the time required for the lens-cap removal and replacement, to control the exposure time, I achieved the most exquisitely detailed photographs of the moment when the life force fled my subjects. You, dear reader, will never know the feeling of absolute power that I possess as the final breath leaves a body – unless, of course, you too are a connoisseur of death.

In July 1855, I collected the details of the demise of a cat and her litter of five kittens – each dispatched in an individual manner. Although the one I subjected to ether gave little resistance and died far too quietly, the adult feline put up an admirable struggle against the death of a thousand cuts. I had read about this in the *Gentleman's*

Magazine (borrowed from Papa's study), in an article on Chinese torture. Sadly, the cat succumbed after only four-hundred-and-twenty-eight cuts, so I may have made the incisions a little too deep, but practice makes perfect: it will be better next time. But I was tiring of animal specimens and determined to move on to larger game.

My brother Nigel was always a hindrance to my studies. He was two years older than I and heir to our father's estates – one day he would become Lord Grosvenor-Berkeley of Heaton Magna – unless fate or I intervened. I was not especially interested in inheriting the title, or even the considerable estates, but the house held so many of my secrets. I did not want him ripping out the Jacobean panelling in the dining room, or having new tiles laid in the dairy, or removing books from the shelves in the library, all of which would reveal certain elements of my collection. Perhaps the greatest inconvenience of youth was that we shared a bedchamber. This caused considerable difficulties with the preparation of specimens. No matter how often I begged Mama to grant me a room of my own in the ramshackle east wing of the house, she would not hear of it.

By the 31st July 1861, I had determined a means of ridding myself of the encumbrance of an elder brother and roommate. On the 6th August, I not only attained my sixteenth year of age but became my father's heir – a birthday gift to myself which gave me inordinate pleasure, even if I did have to conceal it for a while beneath a suitable show of restrained and manly grief. Nigel's body was found after luncheon, in the summer house, seated on the green-painted bench with his favourite author's new book in his hands. Such an irony that it was *Great Expectations* by Charles Dickens – not to my taste at all with a supposed hero so pathetic and lack-lustre; I later took a liking to Conan Doyle's *Sherlock Holmes* stories, the inept efforts at detection proving quite diverting on a dull day. Nigel appeared to have fallen asleep over his reading, but his rest was eternal. I had made sure of that. A weak heart was the cause, as concluded by the coroner after Doctor Pritchard had performed an uninspiring *post-mortem*.

Pritchard never noticed the minute spot on the back of the neck, under the hair, where I had inserted the longest of Mama's hatpins into the point at which the brain stem enters the spinal column. Nigel had been so intent upon his book – as he always was for an hour after luncheon – he was quite unaware of my approach. It was a pity that death was instantaneous and he never knew of its coming. It would have been most informative to have had him die by some gradual means, to have watched the transition from life at the moment of death, but I did not have the leisure for something more meaningful. I simply wiped away the blood speck from his neck, cleaned the hatpin on a leafy plant nearby and returned it to Mama's hatpin cushion in her boudoir. Because death came in an instant, there was no bleeding nor bruising to betray the means.

Nigel was my first human subject.

I began a new collection of *modi operandi*. Avoiding detection is an art and science combined and the police, requiring evidence to be served upon a platter to them, always look to the means of death to solve the case. They are firm believers that every practitioner of crime has his favoured method, whether safe-breaking or pick-pocketing or, in my case, murder. That is why they will never catch me: because I am a collector and no two of my dispatches are ever the same.

Papa's death was such a disappointment to me. My father was intending to have a professional librarian employed to catalogue the extensive library at our residence on Primrose Hill outside London. Clearly, I could not permit such an exercise as might uncover certain items of my early collecting. I had everything planned to perfection for Papa's demise, for not only had I but lately reached my majority at the age of one-and-twenty but the shooting season of 1866 had recently commenced. My father would die in an unfortunate shooting 'accident' while I was elsewhere with an unimpeachable alibi. Every last detail was arranged and, being of age, there would be no reason to delay my full inheritance and, thus, my cancellation of the cataloguing of the library.

Papa always used his favourite Westley-Richard shotgun and I had blocked off both barrels by a most cunning means of pouring molten wax into them, such that my tampering would go unnoticed. When he fired it, it would explode in his face, killing him but, since the heat of the powder blast would melt the wax blockage, clearing the barrels, my efforts would never be known. At least, I hoped that would be the case. These were early days in my career and I admit I lacked a degree of finesse in my work.

Yet it was entirely concomitant with my father's disobliging nature that he thwarted my plan utterly. For one, he used a new shotgun, a Purdey, loaned to him by one of his companions, instead of his usual weapon. Meanwhile, I was at Covent Garden, sharing a box with the Prince of Wales at a performance of Herr Mozart's *The Magic Flute* – although opera was no more to my taste than it was to Bertie's, the female company came royally recommended. As we left the theatre, I was informed by a telegram from my father's grief-stricken shooting companions that he had been consuming a fine salmon supper after a tiring day, spent bagging numerous birds in the most tediously repetitive manner, when a fish bone caught in his throat. This caused him to choke most violently which, in turn, brought on a paroxysm and an ensuing stoppage of the heart. The wretch was dead and all my efforts had served no purpose whatsoever. You may well imagine my abject desolation, dear reader.

It proved, nonetheless, convenient that others interpreted my distress as that of inconsolable grief, rather than intense frustration.

I disposed of Mama some years later – the autumn of 1872, I believe it was, but I should check my records to be certain – by re-distilling her laudanum, so it was trebled in strength. She died in her bed at our residence at Primrose Hill. Her funeral was such a well-attended affair; even the Prince of Wales came to pay his respects.

CHAPTER 1

Saturday, 29th Sept 1888
Whitechapel, London

I HAD so enjoyed my evening at the music hall and was singing one of the more amusing ditties to myself as I strolled along. It was late but the night was not cold, and the earlier rain clouds had dispersed, leaving a fitful moon to light my way, as well as the occasional spluttering gas lamp burning at street corners. Even so, Whitechapel was an obnoxious place of vermin-ridden alleyways and sewer-stinking courtyards. No place for one such as I, you may think, dear reader, yet its very unwholesomeness intrigued me.

The dregs of London's inhabitants were here: petty criminals, alcoholics, foreigners, scroungers and misfits, alongside those who laboured at the docks or in the filthy local industries, sweatshops and workhouses. And the most desperate of all were the street-walkers, tuppenny prostitutes who sold their bodies for a tot of gin. Even so late in the evening of a Saturday, there was no rest for these whores and they lurked beneath the gas lamps – if they were reasonable looking – or in shadowed alleys, if they were haggard, pox-riddled, old and toothless. These were the haunts of thieves and murderers too.

One, in particular, was coming to be known as 'Jack the Ripper', sensationalised by newspapers in search of greater sales. His crimes were gory indeed but lacking in finesse or any inkling of imagination.

Outside the music hall, I had spoken with a woman well into her middle age. A prostitute, obviously, she stank of drink and earlier customers for her disgusting trade. Yet something about her caught my interest.

'You were not born in London, were you?' I said. 'Nor even England, if my ear serves me.'

'Nay, sir. I came from Sweden long ago, in my youth. Then I was Elizabeth Gustafsdottir.' The woman laughed. 'Too much of a mouthful that, so they call me Lizzie Longstride, seeing I walk fast. Mostly to avoid them Blue Devils, if you take my meaning, sir.' She winked her eye and laughed again. 'You willin' to buy a girl a drink first or do you want to get down to business straight? I know a nice secluded alleyway close by.'

'No. I have no interest in that. However, I'll buy you a gin since I should enjoy a drink myself. I have heard that the *Queen's Head* public house dispenses a palatable brew. Shall we?'

I escorted Lizzie as if she was my mother – and indeed she was nigh old enough to be so – to the public house in question. In truth, I had no interest in the disgusting liquor they might pass off as beer in such a den of depravity, but I had something else in mind. A little research was in hand and Lizzie seemed just the kind of whore who might suit my investigations. The sort who would appeal to Jack the Ripper.

The public house was crowded on a Saturday night.

The smoke from countless tobacco pipes and a poor excuse for a coal fire made it hard to see, the gaslights merely illuminating the yellow indoor fog. It was raucous and stinking but, on the whole, the inhabitants of this squalid den were good-natured enough. We squeezed into a corner, Lizzie having sent a couple of young dockers packing, saying she had business to conduct at their table. Me, dear reader: I was the business she proposed. They departed, but the stink of their sweat lingered after. As Lizzie drank her gin and I pretended to sip the odious contents of a greasy tankard, I watched the company.

'So what's a fine gentleman like you doing in Whitechapel, eh?' she asked.

'I attended the music hall,' I replied. As if it was any business of hers.

'Oh. We do get a few toffs now an' then. I know how to give them a good time, for sure. I can play the lady, if you want? Some like that, they do.'

'No doubt.' In error, I let a little of the bilge water in my tankard slip past my lips and almost choked on it. I was watching a youngish fellow through the smoke. He was constantly glancing our way, though whether at me or my companion, I could not at first tell. He was better dressed than the rest – apart from myself, of course – wearing a fairly decent hounds-tooth jacket and a Homburg. Most others here wore shabby workmen's caps. His collar and cuffs looked freshly laundered and starched; his neckcloth was appropriately tied and secured with a tasteful gold pin. He continuously referred to his timepiece, taking it from his waistcoat pocket and returning it to its nest. It seemed to be more of a nervous tic than a concern for the hour. His good quality shoes were recently polished and not overly worn. Comfortable. The word described both his attire and his lifestyle. He was somewhat familiar to me; I had seen him before, though the time and location eluded me for the present.

Yet something was amiss. Belying his general appearance of unexceptional affluence was the look in his eyes. They were not the eyes of a man of culture and restrained temperament. I had seen such a look once before – in the eyes of a dog my father once shot. The creature had begun attacking sheep on our estates and was quite mad. Now that feral glint regarded us across the smoky taproom of the *Queen's Head*. I suspected that I might have found what I sought – if the fellow was observing Lizzie.

Three gins later, Lizzie determined it was time to ply her trade and earn a bed for the night and, if not with me, then with some other customer.

'Well, sir? What's it to be? I can't spend no more time with you unless you're going to be forthcoming with... you know.' She rubbed her finger and thumb together, indicating money.

It was after midnight when we left the public house together. She turned in one direction and I, having bidden her a courteous 'Good evening' and tilted my opera hat, went the other. But briefly, for I withdrew into a shadowed doorway and watched as Lizzie strode away. As I suspected would be the case, the man in the hounds-tooth jacket came from the public house, a package beneath his arm, and glanced both ways. I was unsurprised when, espying the woman, he followed her, keeping to the wall, avoiding the gas lamps. I did the same, though with far greater efficiency of movement and greater skill at concealment.

A 'Blue Devil', as Lizzie had called them, passed me by upon his beat. He bade me 'Good night, sir' and commented that it was a fine evening before touching his helmet and continuing on his way. How dare he speak to me so familiarly! Were it not for the requirement of discretion, I would report the fellow to Commissioner Charles Warren at my club, personally – all men of rank in the Metropolitan Police were members, although I avoided their kind, socially. Their general ineptitude and stupidity were beneath contempt. Instead, I felt relief as the constable's bootsteps, rhythmic on the cobbles, faded into the distance.

Lizzie and the man had turned the corner into Berner Street and were out of my sight for a few minutes. Acknowledging the policeman had delayed me and, when I turned the corner, my quarry had disappeared. No matter. They could not have gone far.

I came upon them in Dutfield's Yard, a fenced enclosure where a solitary gas lamp burned fitfully, shedding a sickly light upon the sordid spectacle. Lizzie lay sprawled at the fellow's feet. Life was already extinct as he, knife in hand, knelt there, hacking at her still-warm flesh.

'What kind of fool are you?' I asked him, leaning back against the paling fence to observe, arms folded. 'Do you not realise that the beat policeman will be returning shortly?'

The man jumped back from his gory work, ready to flee or use his weapon upon his discoverer.

'Fear not,' I said. 'I should be content to teach you but here is not the place. Come. Leave her. We shall find another subject and I will show you how to perform the task more efficiently and without the risk of interruption. You ought to have made use of your watch and timed the policeman's route before making a beginning. Come now. The hour grows late.'

'Who are you?' he enquired warily, wiping his blade clean on Lizzie's tattered petticoats.

'Merely an interested party. You call yourself 'Jack the Ripper' but, in truth, that is no more your name than it is mine.'

He stared at me, wondering whether he should trust me. And then it came to me, where I had seen him.

'I saw you with Adolphus Williamson, the Chief

Constable, did I not, at St John's in Mayfair? And what would such a one as you be doing in a club so exclusive? You must be related to Williamson for I discern a familial likeness about the eyes. That is the case, isn't it?'

'You won't tell Uncle Dolly, will you?' He whined like a naughty child found out in his mischief.

I laughed.

'I have no cause to assist the Metropolitan Police. In fact, I derive a degree of pleasure from observing them in their utterly incompetent confusion. Why would I solve their puzzles for them? You can trust me.'

'I suppose you wonder why I do this,' he said as we hurried away from Berner Street.

'Not at all. Your motives do not interest me.

'My mother and my aunt treat me like a child. I hate them.'

'Why not kill them, in that case? Remove what you loathe.'

'They're both Uncle Dolly's sisters. Can't you imagine the outcry? The entire police force would be on the case.'

I shook my head.

'And you think that would aid them in uncovering the killer – you? There would simply be more policemen getting in each other's way; more useless theories to muddy the waters and create confusion. I should relish the spectacle. But look. We are forgetting the night's business. Over there; see the woman in the paisley shawl and apron? Your next victim, I believe.'

She stood beneath a gas lamp, a plump, middle-aged woman wearing an unfashionable hat.

'Wearing an apron? Is she a prostitute or a charwoman?'

'Does it matter?'

'I prefer it if they're whores.'

'At this hour of the night? What else should she be? Are you having second thoughts now? Unwarranted pangs of conscience of a sudden? Give me your knife; I'll show you how best to do it.' I strolled across to her, touching my hat as I approached her. The knife I kept concealed beneath my evening cape.

'Madam, you look somewhat at a loss. May I escort you home, knowing how dangerous these streets can be?'

'Very kind, I'm sure, sir,' she slurred, 'But I knows me way to Mitre Square from 'ere. I was waitin' for a friend.'

'Perhaps your friend has been detained. But how unmannerly of me: I ought to introduce myself. Adolphus Williamson, at your service, madam. Shall I walk with you a way? Mitre Square is in this direction, is it not?'

'Kate Eddowes,' she said. 'I fink I've 'eard of you somewheres. Anyways, you look a proper gent, so why not?' With that, she took my arm to steady herself and we turned towards Mitre Square. The fumes of cheap gin arose from her each time she spoke. 'I fink we're being follered,' she whispered, drawing me closer.

'What of it? You have me to protect you, madam.' I too could hear the fellow's footsteps behind us. Incompetent.

'Wot if it's 'im? The one they calls Jack the Ripper? Wot then?

'He shall be no concern of yours, I assure you, not now, at least.'

As we turned the corner into Mitre Square, with a light above us, I swung her about so that I was behind her. It was the work of a moment to draw the blade of the knife across her throat, severing the carotid artery and the windpipe, silencing any cry before it began. I lowered the subject to the ground, removing her shawl and apron.

'You did it!' The stupid fellow ran to me, looking shocked.

'Did you suppose I would not? Do you think you have a monopoly on such acts? Here, hold my cape and I shall demonstrate to you the most efficient procedure for removal of the abdominal organs. That is what you normally do – or attempt to do – is it not?'

'Well, yes, but what about the policeman on this beat?'

'Consult that watch of yours,' I told him as I deftly removed the subject's intestines, womb and left kidney.

'Two-and-twenty minutes after one.'

'Then you have twenty-three minutes to do what you will before he returns here.' I handed him his knife and stepped away from the subject. I retrieved my cape from him and took a silk handkerchief from my pocket in which to wrap the expertly incised kidney, having a use in mind for it. While he hacked at the unlovely face in a fit of insane rage, I took a stick, dipped it in the pool of blood and used it as a pen to write a message on the wall, concerning 'Jews being blamed for nothing'. The words were incorrectly spelt, using appalling syntax that would further confuse those Metropolitan fools.

'I believe you have done enough,' I said, 'The subject is all but unrecognisable now. Leave it be. Let us go in search of some refreshment.'

He came willingly as I led him to the *Black Lion*, a noisome drinking establishment close to the docks. He became increasingly intoxicated, though never incapable; I made certain of that, having no intention of carrying the fool to his destiny. I walked and he stumbled from the public house to the riverside. I found a suitable location where a jumble of sacks and crates were stacked in a narrow alleyway, between a butcher's premises and a warehouse that backed onto a wharf. The stink of tar, tobacco and turpentine was nigh overpowering, hinting at the contents of the warehouse. The slaughterer's stench told well enough of what lay beyond the butcher's door.

'Did you clean the knife properly?' I asked him.

'What?'

'Is your blade wiped clean?'

'I wiped it on her apron.'

'Show it to me.'

He obeyed me. It was the last voluntary act of his existence. I took the weapon and made as if to examine it. Then I inserted it into his heart: a most certain and bloodless means of dispatch. Killing a killer, a novel experience indeed. Such a pity that it was so dark, making it impossible to observe the way death drew a film across his eyes but I was able to feel the moment when life departed as he shuddered and went limp in my arms. That compensated me to a degree for the trouble I had taken with this experiment thus far, but my task was yet incomplete.

It was the work of a moment for me to dextrously pick the inadequate lock on the back door of the butcher's premises with my silver lapel-pin – ever retained for the purpose. Once I had found and lighted an oil lamp to illuminate the place of work, it was apparent, fortuitously, that the fellow kept it well organised – if not in the least clean – and everything I required for my endeavours was to hand. A leather apron, already stinking and stiff with gore, hung on a peg behind the door and served well enough to protect my evening attire. Having removed the clothes from the specimen, retaining the timepiece as a memento – sentimental as I am – I lifted the body onto the butcher's block. With cleaver and bone saw provided, I severed the head at the neck before filleting the subject, boning and jointing it until it appeared human no longer. Once dismembered, it was no more than meat and offal which I put into one of the crates and left outside by the butcher's back door. He would be glad of it and, tomorrow, Jack the Ripper, so-called, would make sausages and minced meat for the denizens of Whitechapel.

Hastening now as the working day would soon commence, I wrapped the bones and head separately in a couple of sacks, stuffing the clothes into another before replacing all the tools I had made use of and removing the apron. Although it was not quite yet dawn, I could hear footsteps and voices beyond the front entrance to the shop and made my exit through the back door just as the butcher, for I presumed it was he, came in at the front. It had been a close run thing, but that served to add spice to the event.

Outside in the alley, by the first glimmers of grey daylight, I weighted the bone sack with a few broken bricks and a length of piping before flinging it off the wharf, as far out into the oily waters of the Thames as my considerable strength allowed. It barely made a splash. As for the head, by which the subject might still be identified, I took it with me, to the warehouse next door, finding a way in between two loosened slats in the wooden wall.

It was dark as Hades within, but my nose led me to the barrels filled with tar. As my sight grew accustomed, I could just make out a barrel standing apart from the rest. My questing hand found the reason: the lid was improperly secured. The perfect place. The head sank slowly into the blackness, the tar fumes eye-watering in intensity. With the lid replaced, I departed as I had entered. I washed the blood from my hands in a horse trough. Only the clothes remained to be disposed of: the final evidence of my most recent experiment.

Dawn was breaking in the east, downriver, silhouetting the forest of masts and rigging in the Pool of London against a pink-tinged sky. There were now numerous scabrous, ragged people about, running to their places of employment while the denizens of the night slunk away, into their holes and hovels, to sleep through the daylight hours. A queue of dockers awaited on the wharf, hoping for a day's labour. Such an unsavoury crowd of rascals, I would not give a single one of them the time of day, but I suppose someone has to load and unload the commodities from across the Empire.

As I walked, I noted a propensity of rag-and-bone

merchants in the area and, one by one, threw the items of clothing into their yards, spreading the last evidence of a night's fine work among the buyers and sellers of cast-off clothing. I retained the knife for possible future use. As for the watch, beneath a gas lamp, I examined it more closely. Of fine silver-smith's work, it bore the legend: *To Thomas, on your coming of age, from Uncle Dolly.*

~

I read with much amusement in the following day's edition of *The Times* of the murders of Lizzie Longstride in Dutfield's Yard and Kate Eddowes in Mitre Square. How diverting to learn that Scotland Yard thought the perpetrator of the latter's death might well be a surgeon since he made such a neat job of extracting the whore's organs. Of course, I have been refining the art of death for so long... As for the nigh-illiterate message written on the wall by Jack, that was not mentioned. I wonder why? But then neither was the kidney that I had sent in an elegant box to Inspector Abbeline for his breakfast.

~

I am currently engaged in my next two acquisitions. I exercise my hands daily, strengthening the fingers, for I intend a bare-handed strangulation, though I have not yet selected a subject. That pleasure lies a little in the future. My second acquisition will be quite novel for I intend that it shall be a suicide and, just to make it a little more piquant, one of Scotland Yard's own will be the subject, though I have not yet determined which of two possibilities shall be selected. This project will take time to come to fruition for the specimen for this experiment must be reduced to the most depressing of circumstances so that he will do as I desire. It will be intriguing to discover the method of dispatch that he will choose.

CHAPTER 2

Monday, 8th October 1888.
Scotland Yard

ALBERT SUTTON, as his wife warned every new acquaintance, did not suffer fools gladly. Having been posted by *Those Upstairs* to assist Inspector Abberline on the so-called 'Ripper Case', Inspector Sutton had the feeling he was about to have to suffer a good many fools with a desperate absence of gladness. Frederick Abberline was rummaging through a sheaf of dog-eared and tea-stained reports on his desk, squinting at them; his spectacles pushed up on his sparse hair, forgotten as usual.

'I had it here not five minutes since... accursed reports... too much paper...' Abberline's frayed cuff caught the rim of his teacup, adding more brown splashes to dapple the paperwork. 'Come back later, Sutton, when I've had time to sort out this – this chaos. Always chaos in this job.' He smiled lamely, the lines of weariness etched deep around his mutton-chop moustache. 'I'll have it for you by three of the clock, barring any further unforeseen, er, incidents.'

Sutton knew his colleague was referring to the dreaded possibility of another murder in Whitechapel. On Sunday last, two unfortunate women had been slain and at least two others before that, all attributed to the same – as yet unidentified – perpetrator. Sutton had only been on the case since Friday, spending all day Saturday and his time after church yesterday reading up on the case – or cases. To his mind, the murder of Catherine Eddowes, the supposed fourth victim, killed on 30th September, did not quite fit the pattern.

For one thing, it had been the second 'Ripper' attack on that Sunday night. Fred Abberline had stated that having been disturbed from his first victim, the perpetrator had hurriedly sought out a second to slake his thirst for blood. But particular attention had been given to the 'surgery' carried out on Eddowes – that was the word Dr George Phillips had used to describe what had been done to her corpse – and it displayed 'considerable anatomical knowledge and a level of superior medical skill'.

Secondly, how could that equate with the so-called 'Ripper letters', received prior to the night of double horrors, being written by some barely-literate individual? Abberline had called in hand-writing experts and a doctor from the Bedlam asylum who swore the letters were not only genuine but accorded well with the mental processes of a vicious, ignorant felon from the East End slums. Sutton was perturbed that, in searching Whitechapel and the docks, his fellows at Scotland Yard might well be looking in the wrong place for the murderer, at least as far as the Eddowes case was concerned. This was the reason he needed to see the report of the discovery of a bloodied apron, streets away from the supposed scene of the crime.

'Later, Sutton, I'll find it. Good day to you.'

Just as Albert was about to leave, a young constable knocked on Abberline's door.

'This was delivered for you downstairs, sir. Sergeant Hobhouse told me t' bring it straight up to you.'

Abberline accepted the little parcel and waved the constable away. It was neatly wrapped in brown paper, tied with string, and addressed to 'Inspector F. Abberline, Scotland Yard' in a clear, bold script.

Albert lingered, curious concerning the parcel.

Abberline removed the wrapping. Inside was a pretty enamelled box of the kind a lady might use to keep her jewellery or trinkets. As he opened the lid, a foul stench sent him reeling back, almost tipping his chair over.

'Dear God!' Albert covered his nose with his sleeve. 'What is that thing?'

'A kidney,' Abberline nearly choked on the words. 'And a note... from 'Saucy Jack'. Christ alive! It's Kate Eddowes'...'

Albert always thought he had a strong stomach, but his gorge rose and it required a sterling effort not to embarrass himself by retching where he stood.

'I'll leave you to it,' he said as he hastily took his leave, tipping his hat to Abberline. Not that the man noticed. He was in such a state, too busy mopping up spilt tea and dabbing at his waistcoat with a grubby handkerchief, to no avail. Sutton's courtesy was not essential; the two men were of equal rank but Abberline was a good decade older and under inordinate strain – a little courtesy could do no harm. Hearing the rattle of the teacup as he closed the door made Albert aware that he was badly in need of a restorative to settle his stomach. He had breakfasted with Nell some while since, if a bowl of lukewarm porridge, the colour of a London Particular, could be glorified by the term 'breakfast'. He couldn't blame Nell: raised in the workhouse, what chance had she ever had to learn to cook? She did her best by him, but a visit to Mrs Mumbles' tearoom was definitely in order.

With chintz curtains, lace tablecloths and a good fire in the well-blacked hearth, the tearoom was welcoming on a chilly October morning; a definite reminder that summer was over. Albert removed his hat and set it on the cushioned chair beside him. There was no need to order. Kitty Mumbles knew his requirements. A pot of tea, a round of toast, butter and Dundee marmalade were duly set before him, along with the morning edition of *The Times*. The Whitechapel murders were now just a half column on page four. Albert thanked the Good Lord as he munched his toast: no gruesome headlines today. On page five he noted a brief article concerning a woman who had been approached two nights ago in a dark alley off Buck's Row, scene of the first Ripper murder, by a scruffily-dressed man who spoke 'like a foreigner'. The fellow had been carrying a large leather bag, so she thought, and she 'didn't like the look of him one bit'. Albert thought it might be worth questioning the woman later, so he circled the column with the green crayon that he kept in his pocket for the purpose.

He glanced up from his repast as another customer came in: a man of middle age, impeccably dressed with reddish hair reaching to his spotless collar but attired as though he had just come from the opera. A silk-lined cape, gold-topped cane, lapel-pin and patent evening shoes were a little eccentric for nine o' clock in the morning. Perhaps the gentleman had yet to go home after an evening in the West End.

Their eyes met. The gentleman nodded 'Good day' and smiled a little. Albert returned the gesture but quickly gave his attention to his rapidly-cooling tea, somewhat embarrassed to have been caught staring. It was most unprofessional, not to say ill-mannered. Yet on two occasions as he glanced at the stranger from behind the security of his newspaper, the gentleman was watching him, making no attempt to disguise his rapt gaze. Suddenly feeling like a specimen trapped in an observation jar, Albert left a florin on the table, grabbed his hat and hurried from the tearoom, leaving Kitty Mumbles' queries unheeded.

'Well, I never did!' she said, still looking at the gaping door which the inspector had failed to close as he left. 'What's amiss with him, eh? Not like Inspector Sutton to rush off without a 'thank you' like that. And he forgot his paper.' She set a hearty platter of devilled kidneys and scrambled eggs before the fine gentleman at table three.

'Courtesy is a dying art, I fear, madam,' he replied, smoothing his Macassar-oiled hair, 'Even among the Metropolitan Police, it seems. Would you be so good as to pass me that newspaper which the fellow has discarded? And please close the door: such a chill draught.'

Kitty bobbed a little half curtsey and did as she was asked, then left the customer to eat his meal in peace and browse his newspaper.

CHAPTER 3

THREE YEARS after I had commenced the human branch of my research with Nigel's death, I realised it could be dangerous if my family and servants were my sole specimens. By this time, although Papa and Mama were still breathing, I had accounted for Cousin Lucinda – her ghastly neighing laugh became too much to bear – by means of hemlock in her hot chocolate and my father's irritating valet suffered a fall on the stairs (though I had already broken his neck to make certain of his demise). And then there was the incident with the dairymaid. Whether you believe me or not, it was an entirely fortuitous accident that, having attempted to seduce me with a kiss after following me into the barn, she stumbled when I pushed her away and became impaled upon a pitchfork.

In truth, I had been aroused by the attempted kiss, but her death throes were more enjoyable – most fascinating to observe as she writhed and twitched and shuddered. I was able to watch her eyes as the life force was spent and they glazed over in death. It was all most instructive. I should have had to kill her anyway, once she realised what I had been doing in the barn: disposing of my father's favourite hound, the subject of one of my less successful experiments which had required the use of a galvanic battery and a copper coal scuttle. I shall say no more.

However, with so many subjects expiring in my vicinity, even the most inept policeman might become a little suspicious if matters continued in this way. My time at Eton made things difficult. One was never alone there and I poured my enthusiasm into cricket and rugger instead. But upon my release from the *alma mater*, before going up to Oxford, I determined that the next addition to my collection should be a stranger, taken quite at random from society.

It was on a warm Saturday evening, the 9th July 1864 to be precise, that I finally spread my wings in terms of experimentation. There were hints of an approaching storm - the air close and muggy as a sweaty rugger shirt - and distant grumbling thunder could be heard as I awaited the 9.50 pm train at Fenchurch Street Station. As the locomotive drew in, enveloped in a cloud of steam and sparks, hissing like a ferocious iron snake, an elderly gentleman acknowledged my courtesy with a smile when I allowed him to climb aboard first.

'Think we may be in for a storm, shortly, young man,' he said, 'Let us hope we are within doors before then.'

'Indeed,' I replied, touching my hat.

We were travelling in a first class compartment of a North London Railway train, bound for Highbury. I was intending to visit a cousin, for whom I held little affection, and musing upon the fact that I had never heard of a murder being committed on the railways – accidents aplenty, but never yet a purposeful death. My companion in the carriage was of slight build, attired as a gentleman of the City, complete with a tall silk hat and a gold Albert watch and chain which he frequently consulted, frowning through his gold-rimmed spectacles just as my father did, as though late for an appointment. He clutched a worn leather bag from which protruded a large manila envelope addressed to Messrs Robarts, Curtis & Co in the City of London. Since the envelope had been opened, I concluded – correctly, as it turned out – that he worked for the bank of that name. Beside him on the seat lay a silver-topped walking stick – as fine a weapon as I might have hoped for. What an interesting, indeed unique, addition it would be to my collection – not only a murder by violent, unpremeditated assault but the first ever carried out upon a railway train. The idea intrigued and excited me, but I had the excuse of youth, being still a month shy of having attained my nineteenth birthday.

I timed it so that the locomotive was gathering speed as we left Old Bow station. It was an act of a few moments – no longer – to grab his walking stick, knock his hat aside with it and bring it down upon his skull with all my strength, which was quite considerable due to my sporting activities at Eton so recently ended. For a moment, he stared at me in surprise, but his skull must have been an insubstantial thing for it burst like an overripe fruit. Fortunately, I had stood well back, knowing how freely a head wound will bleed, yet the blood and brains splattered the compartment, soaking the upholstery of the seat and pooling on the floor as he fell forward, soundlessly. Not a groan nor a whimper. His spectacles had fallen on the seat and I removed his watch and chain and left them there with his hat, bag and cane, knowing some fool would be unable to resist temptation and thus incriminate themselves with a murdered man's possessions. Before we slowed on approaching Victoria Park and Hackney Wick station, I opened the carriage door and kicked his limp form out, onto the track. I made no attempt to check that he was dead: if he were not then the next train would attend to the matter.

I alighted at Victoria Park while the train steamed

on towards Chalk Farm, took a Hansom to the West End and partook of a fine supper. The visit to my cousin could await some other tedious evening in need of an element of interest. Over brandy, I wrote up a detailed report on my latest addition to the collection. I could not put a name to my new acquisition until Monday morning when *The Times* carried the story of Mr Thomas Briggs, Chief Clerk at the Bank of Robarts, Curtis & Co. found unconscious beside the railway track – a letter in his pocket had served to identify the victim. He was taken to a local public house, *The Mitford Castle* in Cadogan Terrace, but had died last evening without being able to say anything of his attacker. That was a relief to me. I should not make the same error again but always ascertain that death had occurred before discarding a specimen.

As I intended, someone had taken Briggs's belongings and the police, over-eager and foolish as ever, quickly arrested some German fellow, Franz Muller, found to be wearing Briggs's hat and carrying a pawnbroker's ticket for a gold watch and chain. This timepiece, when redeemed by the police, carried an inscription to Thomas Briggs as the long-serving secretary of a Gentlemen's Literary Society. Since the German's alibi consisted of a whore and her madam, it counted for nought. He was tried, convicted and executed at Newgate in the following November.

I do not make a habit of consorting with the multitudinous rabble, but I made an exception to attend his hanging, to pay my respects and to add another unexpectedly fortuitous specimen to my collection. I made careful notes and detailed drawings of his dispatch which was fairly gratifying. My observations could have been enhanced considerably had it not been for the absurd tradition of the condemned being required to wear a bag over their head. Was this to spare the squeamish, I always wondered? Surely that made little sense, for was it not to witness a gruesome spectacle that the crowd gathered in such numbers? Why hide from them the very moment of death which they came to view? I could but think that it was the authorities themselves, those who had passed the sentence of justice, who had not stomach enough to see through to its climax the due process of law that they had set in motion.

CHAPTER 4

Wednesday, 10ᵗʰ October

ALBERT STOOD, looking down at the mud. Westminster Bridge was just a dark presence in the fog to his right. Sounds from the street were muted: a distant call, the faint clop of hooves and trundling wheels of a Hansom cab on the bridge. Evening came early in such weather. Below him, the river water sucked and slobbered at the tidal rubbish. He could not help but recall yesterday's greasy ox-tail soup, served up by Nell, full of unnameable bits of offal, though he had examined each piece before eating it, to make certain it wasn't kidney. But the river smelled even worse. He shivered as tendrils of fog tickled at the back of his neck beneath his hat.

'What am I looking at, constable?' The beam of a bull's-eye lantern swung across the ooze at the water's edge, alighting on some thin, pale object.

'Here, Mr Sutton, sir,' Constable Michaelson's voice was somewhat muffled in the thickening fog. 'A leg, sir: a woman's, I reckon.'

Sighing over the likely ruination of yet another pair of decent leather shoes, Albert went down the weed-strewn steps, taking care not to slip. Irreparable damage to his footwear was bad enough; a similar fate for his dignity in front of a wet-behind-the-ears constable would be insupportable. Thames mud clung to his feet and trouser-bottoms before he had gone two yards. Nell would despair of getting them clean again.

Setting the problems of his meagre wardrobe aside, Albert crouched by the object. He pulled aside a short length of rope which had tangled around it and picked away the evil-smelling weed, startled when some living thing scuttled off.

'Sweet Lord save us! The rats are bold as street-walkers, constable.'

'Yes, sir. Brazen buggers they are, as you say. I brung a sack, sir, like you told me to.'

'Well done. Is it clean?'

'I shaked all the spuds out of it and the dirt, best I could, sir.'

'Then it will have to do. It can give no offence to the woman now, fine lady as she once was.'

'How d'you know that, sir? How can you tell what she was, just by seeing her leg?'

'The buttoned boot on the end of it, constable: hand-stitched and little worn. The remnants of woollen stocking are of the finest denier. And no sign of wear upon the knee. She never knelt to scrub a floor or polish a hearthstone. Now assist me in getting it into the sack, then you can take it over the bridge, to Dr Philips at St Thomas's. I will see you back at the Yard by a half after eight for a full report as to how you found it.'

'Is it another Ripper job, you think, sir?' Constable Michaelson had asked as they wrapped the leg respectfully as they could in the potato sack. Albert dusted off his hands and shook his head. His knee cracked as he stood up, loud enough that he worried the constable might have heard it.

'No. No similarities as far as I can make out but Dr Philips will be able to tell us more. This is hardly the Ripper's stamping ground, is it? And far too close to home for us. It may be connected to what was unearthed on Tuesday last, in the digging of the foundations for our new building, though it seems rather fresh to be a week old or more.'

'You mean the body in the black dress? That were a gruesome find, sir, no mistake. Nearly lost me breakfast when I seed it, sir.'

'Indeed, constable, but I think that is quite sufficient idle speculation until we know more. Now get that sack to St Thomas's in haste. Here, take three pence for a Hansom cab.'

The constable led the way, back up the treacherous water stairs, the sacking-wrapped bundle under one arm, the lantern in his left hand. Four steps up and he was already disappearing in the sulphurous-yellow murk and deepening darkness. Albert tried consulting his pocket watch but the feeble glow of the gas lamps by Westminster Bridge did not reach so far and he could not make out the hands on the mother-of-pearl face, no more than a pale disc in the night.

Nevertheless, his stomach suggested it was time for an early supper. Despite his hunger, his wife Nell's cast-iron piecrust and stringy, grey meat – her best efforts at a mutton pie – held no temptation for him. He would use his work as an excuse to avoid her cooking, yet again. Much as he adored her, there were limits as to what he could endure swallowing and Nell's promised supper was a step beyond. With a sigh and a sudden rush of anticipatory saliva to his tongue, he thought of Kitty Mumbles' chicken and leek soup with savoury dumplings. There was probably just time, if he hurried, before the tearoom closed at a quarter after seven.

Still contemplating the delights of Mrs Mumbles' supper to come, Albert groped his way through the thickening fog. The cobbles were greasy and slick with horse-dung, mud and other gutter-slime and once he slipped and almost fell into a pile of ordure, the work of a street-sweeper making an early start on his night's work. The fellow, oblivious to Albert's near-mishap, went on, pushing his broom and whistling tunelessly in the gloom. Within a few steps, the small sound was swallowed by the mist and all other night-time noises were muffled and distorted. The jingle of harness might have been imagined as Albert could hear no accompanying clop of hooves. He instinctively looked both ways before crossing the road towards the tearoom, but there were only swirling blankets of yellow vapour on either hand, hanging like grubby laundry on unseen washing lines. He coughed as the taint of sulphur and soot caught in his throat.

At that moment, he was flung aside like a rag, falling through the air for what seemed like minutes, until the wet pavement rushed up to meet him at the speed of a steam locomotive. He put out his hands to save himself but a searing pain shot up his right arm as he crunched against the foot of a wall, knocking the breath out of him. In the silence which followed, the dark shape of a carriage vanished into the night and Albert was sure he heard laughter, but his senses were spiralling away, becoming one with the fog that shrouded him.

~

'Thank goodness for that, Mr Sutton. You had us all quite worried, sir.' The voice was feminine and familiar, but it took Albert a moment or two to place it: Kitty Mumbles. He stirred, feeling cushions beneath him. Every bone hurt and somewhere a more demanding pain nagged at him, but he could not decide quite where it was. Or where *he* was.

'Lie easy, Mr Sutton. You've had quite a knock. I heard the thud as you hit my front wall. Charlie, the street-sweeper, helped get you inside. Now he's gone to fetch the doctor. Here, let me help you. Drink this: it's cherry brandy.'

'Mustn't... drink... on duty.' Albert could hear his own words slurring like a drunkard's. 'No doctor... don't need...'

'I can't agree with you, Mr Sutton.' A gentle hand was wiping his brow with something wet and cool. It smelled of *eau de cologne*. Then it was gone and he felt the rim of a glass pressed to his lips. 'Sip a little, sir: it will revive you.' Syrupy and fiery, the cherry brandy slid down easily and his wandering senses began to gather themselves.

'Where am I?'

'My back parlour, sir. Couldn't leave you outside, could we? Nor have you bleeding on the tearoom floor.'

'Bleeding?'

'You have a lump the size of a hen's egg and still growing on your forehead. It may need stitching; that's why Charlie's gone for the doctor. And your wrist doesn't look quite right either. I think it could be broken.'

'Oh.'

For a while, he lay back, trying to get the cushions just so. The bump on his forehead throbbed horribly. Was he getting blood on the cushions? Did he care if he was? He could hear Kitty Mumbles moving around the room but, other than spreading a quilt over him, she left him undisturbed.

'What happened to me? Do you know?' he asked when he heard the sound of a teacup being stirred.

'Charlie said he thought it was a carriage what ran you down, but he couldn't make much of it in this fog. You can ask him when he gets back with the doctor. Shouldn't be long now; he only lives two streets away. Mind you, in this weather...'

Albert lost the rest of the conversation as he dozed

on the couch, thinking he should have taken more care, crossing the thoroughfare; wondering if they'd let him work with a broken wrist – if it was – how would he write up his reports? And Nell... he must let her know... later. Best not to worry her unnecessarily. Someone ought to reprimand that carriage driver, travelling so fast in the fog with no lamps showing, laughing. And in his mind's eye, he could see a peculiar bird, or a beast was it? He had seen it before, somewhere.

CHAPTER 5

I WAS at my club of St John's in Mayfair, writing up my journal, noting the details of an earlier experiment. I had poisoned a fellow on Paddington Station, giving him my hip-flask of brandy when he felt unwell as we waited for the Windsor train. He was a complete stranger, but his cravat was distasteful and singled him out. He felt a good deal worse after drinking the brandy-foxglove mixture, though the station-master commended me upon my act of kindness in assisting the man, even as his heart was giving out. I added it as Experiment Number Twenty-Eight in the section on 'Poisonings'.

'Your brandy, my lord.' The butler made the most minuscule of bows as he hovered by my armchair in the club's library. 'Dinner will be served at your request, in the private dining room in a quarter of an hour, sir.'

'Make certain the beef is rare, not some blackened burnt offering, like last time.'

'Very good, my lord. I'll have a word with the cook.'

'See that you do.'

When he had departed on silent feet, I smiled to myself, looking back to an earlier entry in my journal. Number Twenty-Three had been a most satisfying experiment concerning a steak-and-kidney pudding, here at my club, one which I laced with a poison of unusual origin.

In the *Gentleman's Magazine,* I had read an article about a tribe in the Amazonian jungle of South America who used the secretions of a species of tree-frog to tip their arrows – a deadly toxin, apparently. Intrigued, I had arranged, at great expense, to have half a dozen of these fascinating amphibians imported from Brazil. *Phyllobates terribilis* – such a marvellous name, you will agree – proved to be no larger than my thumbnail and a most exquisite golden colour. The combination of such beauty and deadliness appealed to me. Each tiny frog exuded sufficient poison to kill ten men, so my research revealed, and gathering the substance had to be done with extreme care.

It still gave me a frisson of pleasure, remembering how I had disguised myself as a humble delivery man in dusty coat and ragged cap, leaving a sack full of onions in the scullery behind the club. Using the tradesmen's entrance was a new experience, touching my cap to a lowly cook was another. It was then the work of an instant to smear a few drops of poison onto the suet, grated and ready to go into the pastry. It had to be in the pudding itself, not the filling, because any half-decent cook, worthy of the title, would taste the filling before it went into the pastry, to check the seasoning. I had no wish to add the cook to my collection and, besides, if he died too soon, my intended specimens – my fellow club members – would never get to eat their deadly repast.

That Wednesday evening, I observed with barely concealed jubilation as others ordered the pudding. I myself chose the fricassee of rabbit. My well-conceived plan was a complete success: eighteen members fell ill within two hours of dining and the death rate was most pleasing.

The Honourable William Platt MP even survived long enough for me to attend his deathbed the next morning, for

I was eager to observe the effects of the expensive poison. Platt could not speak as the poison paralysed the muscles and death came by suffocation as the specimen could no longer draw breath. It was not an especially interesting death, as I had hoped, but an efficient method of dispatch – since ten of the eighteen succumbed – and quite undetectable. Of the survivors, two never made a full recovery and both were added to my collection before the year was out. I appeared of woeful countenance at the funerals of all my fellow club members as had selected the steak-and-kidney pudding for dinner on that fateful Wednesday. It was always going to be upon a Wednesday: the menu at St John's Club being as unalterable as death itself.

However, poisons as a means of dispatch were beginning to pall, so I wanted something new – loving novelty as I do, it becomes difficult at times to be always original – so my present challenge excites me. The act of initiating death is not sufficient any longer to set my blood racing. Like a huntsman, the chase has become as important – if not more so – than the kill. The identification, the stalking of the selected quarry and then that sublime moment, the shock when it realises it has become the prey, when it knows it must fight or flee, the instant of terror when it can no longer do either and confronts death. Some look death in the eye, angry at their failure, others turn away, pathetic and whimpering. I find it illuminating to study these responses, cataloguing them, but there are few alternatives. I long to observe a unique response to the final, intimate subjection to death. Perhaps my next specimen will provide one; I have high hopes for my most recent selection.

I had already commenced my new experiment while driving my brougham myself tonight, here to my club, through the fog. There is quite an art to finding one's way on such an evening but my driver is not privy to my collecting activities and I gave him the night off, though he tried to persuade me otherwise, fearing I might wreck the carriage, I suppose. I doubt he was truly concerned for my safety.

The butler's soft cough drew my attention – his soundless tread could be quite unnerving and might require action be taken at some time in the near future. I flexed my fingers, considering whether he might be worthy of their power as a means of death. His skinny neck hardly looked to require a deal of effort. Mayhap a snapped vertebra would prove more instructive than strangulation? But that may be too swift an end for I felt the need to make him suffer. A bullet wound to the abdomen, perhaps. I would study the matter more deeply before making my decision.

'Dinner is served, my lord,' the butler said grandly, as though announcing the arrival of King Solomon himself.

I drained my brandy and rose to make my way into the intimacy of the private dining room. The new gas lamps shed a golden glow over red velvet draperies, heavy with tobacco smoke and ancient snuff, which some members still favoured. The brass firedogs gleamed in the hearth and a sudden settling of coals sent sparks spiralling up the chimney. I took my seat at my usual table, set with finest white linen, silver cutlery and crystal glasses. A table for one, of course. I never shared a meal with anyone and my fellow diners knew better than to invite me to their table, or to interrupt my private cogitations with meaningless words. These were reasons why I liked St John's; it suited my tastes and needs admirably.

Over roast beef and roast potatoes, I thought upon my thirty years of experimentation and the next stage of the pursuit of my present quarry. I did not suppose, as yet, that the specimen realised he was under observation, despite my scrutiny of him at breakfast in that common little teashop the other morning. He most certainly was not upon his guard or this evening's encounter with my brougham would not have been possible – an amusing little diversion, nothing more; a piquant dash of sauce to add flavour to a dish. I smeared horseradish on my rare beef and wondered how Inspector Sutton was recovering from his moment of misadventure by Westminster Bridge.

I could but hope he had appreciated my little gift to him earlier: a rather elegantly-stockinged leg. If he has wit enough, he will be able to marry it up with the other body parts I have scattered about the environs of London to entice and tease the Metropolitan Police. I even left the torso, neatly wrapped, amid the construction site of Scotland Yard's own new building. How much more aid do the fools require? The whole ensemble was previously known as the Honourable Beatrice de Quincy-Bascombe, yet I doubt they will ever unravel that little mystery. The girl was feeling rather unwell that day last month when we strolled through Green Park. She had a most unpleasant cough that quite got on one's nerves and simply had to be silenced. The old trick with the hatpin – supplied by Beatrice herself – proved as efficacious as it had with dear Nigel all those years before.

CHAPTER 6

**Thursday, 11th October
6, Summerlea Villas, Carlisle Place,
near Victoria Station**

'**O**H, NELL, my dearest, another disaster?'

The acrid smell of a burnt supper had assaulted Albert's nostrils as soon as he came through the front door.

'I'm so sorry,' Nell sobbed, dabbing at her reddened eyes with the corner of her apron. 'I'm sorry I'm such a useless wife to you. I'm no good at anything.'

Albert took his stick-thin wife in a tender embrace, mindful of his injured arm, and stroked her hair.

'That is nonsense, Nell, as you well know. Do I not come home each day to a spotless house, shirts so white they dazzle the eye and all impeccably starched and ironed? Are not the fires always lit, the shelves dusted and the rugs thoroughly beaten? Most important of all: am I not welcomed with a loving kiss and a bright smile... usually? Come, where is that smile today, eh?' He held her at arms' length, waiting until her lips twitched into a more pleasing shape, if not quite the smile he wished to see. He took out his handkerchief from the top pocket of his tweed jacket and wiped away the tear-stains on her pale cheeks. 'There: that looks better.'

'But I burnt the shepherd's pie. There's nothing for supper, Albert. I just can't get used to using a range, judging how long things take to bake or boil or roast. It's always either raw or black as a cinder. I don't...'

'Hush, dearest. Put on your best dress: tonight I will take you out to supper. Tomorrow, I will place an advertisement in *The Times* for a cook...'

'But the expense...'

'I am an inspector now; we can afford someone to come in, to prepare and serve the meals. Come, let me see you in the blue dress, the one which reflects the summer skies in your eyes.'

Nell giggled:

'More like rainy October clouds in my eyes tonight.'

Nell rushed upstairs to change and Albert went to open the kitchen window to let out the smell of his burnt supper. But the open window let in the cold and a sleek black shape came through like a shadow on the draught. It landed on the draining board with a plaintive 'meow'.

'If you're hungry, Blackstock, you can eat this shepherd's pie,' Albert told the cat, setting the enamel dish on the floor. The cat sniffed at it, patted the dish with its paw and turned its back. 'I agree with you for once,' he said as the cat stalked off, into the hallway. 'And don't lie on the stairs in the dark, hoping to trip me up either.'

Blackstock was in the habit of sprawling the full width of a stair in the gloom of the stairwell, his black shape invisible. Nell had never come to grief in such circumstances, but Albert had a feeling the cat did it on purpose whenever he was hurrying on the stairs. More than once he'd narrowly missed breaking his neck, having suddenly felt the softness of flesh and fur beneath his foot, trying not to crush the wretched animal and missing the step it had chosen for its bed. Each time he'd tumbled or slipped as he lost his balance but had suffered no injury. One of these days he might not be so lucky.

~

As they left the house a half hour later, taking the omnibus from Victoria Station via Westminster, heading for the gaslit gaiety of Covent Garden, neither noticed the brougham, blinds drawn, following them at a discreet distance. It was mid-October and certainly no Indian summer evening, but at least the fog of the previous night was gone, blown away on a rising westerly that brought the scent of rain. Although it was just dusk, the moon was already visible through the broken clouds, scurrying by like homeward bound commuters eager for a warm fireside. Albert still had a sore head from yesterday's encounter with a carriage. His wrist was badly bruised and swollen and, not wanting to repeat that experience, he took extra care when crossing the busy thoroughfare, having alighted from the omnibus.

Albert chose *Bennett's*, a respectable establishment in Goodwood Place, off Covent Garden. Later it would be crowded when the theatres closed and society-types trooped in for a late supper, decked in their finery, but for now, it was quiet. The proprietor smiled and offered them a table by the window. Albert shook his head, indicating his arm in a sling.

'Of course, sir, a more discreet table at the back, then. Shall I instruct the cook to cut your meat before serving?'

'Thank you, but there will be no need: my wife is

perfectly capable of assisting me if required.' It was pleasing to learn that the man producing the food was a cook, not a *chef.* Albert had no liking for fancy French dishes: all sauces and no substance with ridiculous names which meant you had no idea what would be set before you. It was the reason why he had chosen *Bennett's* with its plain, honest English name. He wasn't disappointed: juicy sirloin with carrots and cauliflower, to be followed by jam sponge pudding and custard.

'Did you manage at work today, Albert?' Nell asked as she cut his beef into bite-sized pieces, 'With your arm, I mean.'

'They've put me on so-called light duties, more's the pity.' He took a sip of stout before Nell put his dinner plate in front of him and he set about his meal. 'Light duties are a joke,' he said, spearing a floret of pale cauliflower, dipping it in gravy and chewing it with pleasure. He swallowed: 'It means I dance attendance on the Chief Superintendent: "fetch this; bring that; file those..." It would be less hard work chasing felons. I barely had time to dash out for a sandwich while 'god' was at luncheon with Lord Someone-or-Other. Are you enjoying your dinner?'

Nell nodded and finished her mouthful:

'It's delicious, thank you. I hope we can come here again.'

~

'I can't eat another mouthful,' Nell said, having scraped the last smear of raspberry jam from the bottom of her bowl, 'But that was the very best I've tasted.'

Albert chuckled: his wife's experience of fine dining was limited to Kitty Mumbles' tearoom. Before that, it had been workhouse gruel with mouldy bread or the Salvation Army soup kitchen twice a week. The first time Nell had seen a joint of meat had been the roast ham Kitty Mumbles laid on for their wedding breakfast. The poor lass had almost swooned with joy at her first taste, going into raptures over what had been a pleasant but hardly extraordinary meal.

'Don't laugh at me, Albert Sutton, or I'll put you on bread-and-water rations. I think you need it.' She poked at his taut waistcoat with her licked-clean spoon, where the buttons strained at the worn cloth. 'I don't know how you stay so plump on my wretched efforts at cooking. I think you must spend half your day at Mrs Mumbles' place.' Albert felt his cheeks redden and hoped Nell wouldn't notice in the subdued light of the gasoliers, hiding his guilt behind his glass of stout as he drained it dry.

~

As they left *Bennett's*, well fed and laughing, Nell hanging on to Albert's good arm, a figure hurried towards them from a dark alleyway, off Goodwood Place.

'Nell! Nell!' someone called out. As the figure came into the gaslight, Nell let go of Albert and went forward. The girl held a near-empty flower-basket with a few sprigs of dried lavender remaining. 'It is you, ain't it Nell?'

'Betsy... how are you?' Nell flung her arms around the shabby girl. 'What are you doing out at this hour?'

'Never mind me. I jus' thought you should know: you two's being follered.'

'What's all this about, then?' Albert sounded too much like a representative of the Metropolitan Police, even to his own ears.

'Albert, this is Betsy Briars, we used to look out for each other when we were...'

'Oh, sir,' Betsy interrupted her old friend's introduction, 'You're being follered, sir. He's been waiting – pretend you're buying a posy off me, sir – he's watching from the corner behind you, by the pillar-box. No! Don't turn round; he'll see you.'

'What makes you think he is following us, Miss Briars?'

'He arrived just after you did, comed from the same direction. I thought it was you, Nell, though in them fine clothes... Anyway, I was waiting to talk to you, jus' to pass the time o' day fer old times' sake, you know... and he waited too, kept looking at his pocket watch and then at the door of *Bennett's*. Then, as you comed out, he dashed round the corner, be'ind that pillar-box, outta sight.'

'Well, thank you, miss,' Albert said loudly, pressing a shilling into Betsy's cold, chapped hand – just as Nell's had once been – and selecting the best bunch of lavender from the few poor ones left in the basket. Quietly he said: 'I'm sure it's nothing to be concerned about. Get yourself a decent bed for the night immediately, miss.'

'Yes, sir. Thanking you, sir. You're very generous, sir.' Betsy bobbed a curtsy as Albert drew Nell away.

'Who could be following us, Albert?' Nell whispered, 'And why do you drag us away? I wanted to talk with Betsy.'

Albert didn't answer but led her around the corner, into the darkness of Lewis Yard and stopped. He removed his hat and peered around the edge of the crumbling brick building, back towards *Bennett's*.

'I think it is more likely to be Betsy who is being followed. The fellow may be stalking his next victim.'

'Oh, God! Albert!' Nell's hands flew to her mouth as if to prevent the dreaded words escaping. 'You mean Jack the Ripper is after Betsy?'

'No, not him, Nell. This is not his stamping ground. All the same, I don't want your friend to be in danger from any villain with evil intent.'

Albert observed the street for a good ten minutes after Betsy had disappeared, but no one followed her. Just a stray dog and an enclosed brougham turning around in the road before heading towards Westminster, a gilded crest of some mythical beast or other on the doors catching the gaslight as it manoeuvred. He thought he might have seen the crest before but maybe not.

CHAPTER 7

Friday, 12th October
6, Summerlea Villas

NELL SAT by the kitchen range – her favourite place in the house when Albert was out, working. Blackstock, her over-fed tomcat, lay sprawled at her feet, soaking up the warmth from the range but Nell knew he wasn't sleeping. His whiskers twitched, his tail curled: the cat was biding his time, certain a few morsels of her midday meal of bread-and-dripping would surely come his way if he was patient.

With a sigh, feeling guilty for making him wait, Nell tore the middle out of her sandwich: the best bit where the mutton dripping was thickest, and held it for Blackstock. He sniffed it carefully, as if it was a great delicacy to be savoured, before wolfing it down, licking his mouth so as not to waste a crumb in his fur. He gazed up at Nell, the artful glint in his peridot-green eyes was absent for once, exchanged for the beseeching look of the starving stray he once had been but belied by the sleek gloss of his sable fur and lithe mouser's body. The pathetic, mewling kitten Nell had found shivering in Blackstock Alley had long since become the king of the neighbourhood and sire of innumerable balls of black fur from Victoria Station to the Palace of Westminster.

Nell gave him the rest of the sandwich, making-do with a second cup of tea for herself.

Having poured the tea, she reached for the milk jug and something caught her eye outside the kitchen window. To the right of the little wash-house, at the bottom of the tiny square of back garden where spotless sheets flapped on the line, stood what they called 'the potting shed'. The previous occupant of the house had been a keen grower of lilies, but now the shed was unused for such things, Albert not knowing one end of a dibber from the other. In the spring, Nell was planning to grow a few vegetables and flowers, but at the moment they kept nothing but Albert's collection of old newspapers in the shed. She noticed that the gate was swung a little ajar – that must have been what she'd seen.

A faint sound caused Blackstock to forget his meal. Fur bristling, tail erect, the tom seemed to double in size. Ears back, teeth bared, he hissed at the kitchen door which led out to the wash-house.

'Whatever is it, Blackstock?' Nell reached out to soothe the animal, but he only backed away, hissing like a steaming kettle on the range. 'It's probably the grocer's boy, delivering my order, though he's rather late today. You don't need to spit at young Dicky; you know him well enough. Now behave yourself, you silly creature.'

But when Nell opened the back door, it wasn't Dicky with a box of groceries. She never saw who it was as a musty-smelling blanket was flung over her head. She tried to fight free of the heavy woollen folds, but strong arms pinned her down. She screamed, but the blanket muffled her cries. She was lifted up and carried outside. Whoever had her in his arms, she felt him stumble on the third tiled step, down into the garden, the one which was loose; the one Albert always intended to mend.

Then she was being lowered. Not to the ground but she sensed being enclosed, heard the blanket snagging on a rough surface. The darkness of the shrouding cloth became more intense, then absolute. The thud of a closing lid, the rasp of metal as a bolt slid home plunged Nell into a moment of shrieking panic, then into a state of silent, rigid fear.

The Grosvenor-Berkeley residence, Primrose Hill

His wife. She is coming. I shall have her. If things went smoothly, without any problems, they would be here any moment. I am so looking forward to this. Not to meeting the snivelling slut, of course, I have no interest in her except for her relationship with him. The fool dotes upon her and her disappearance is going to send him into paroxysms of fear and despair when he fails to find her. How I shall enjoy observing him, making notes upon his deteriorating ability to function, to think logically, to continue to do his work of detecting as he sinks into the abyss of not-knowing.

And how might I deal with her? Perhaps strychnine? No. There is no finesse in that. Maybe I should make a third attempt at the death-of-a-thousand-cuts? How else to perfect the method? My first attempt was that cat, years ago, taking only a couple of hundred or so cuts. My second was at Christmas 1872. I recall that I disguised my height with a severe stoop, wore theatrical makeup to make my skin appear blotched and pimpled and spoke with a most convincing German accent. I picked up a whore, Harriet Buswell (known as Hattie, so she told me), at the *Alhambra Theatre* on Christmas Eve. We took an omnibus back to her dreary lodgings at 12 Great Coram Street, WC1, where, having bound and gagged her, I carried out my second experiment to create a death-by-a-thousand-cuts. This time, it took more than eight hundred cuts to kill her, but I could not be precise as to the moment of death, which was most frustrating. Having made detailed drawings and taken photographs, I divested myself of the well-bloodied dark overcoat, removed the makeup and strode out of the house at a half after six on Christmas morning. How amusing it was to read in *The Times,* in the days following, that the police had busied themselves arresting German seamen, including a padre, although the case remains unsolved to this day.

Ah! I hear them: my minions. They had better have conducted the operation successfully, or they will be joining my collection forthwith as experiments for my next project.

Two tattered fellows in hobnailed boots, caps and leather aprons came into the library, encumbered by a large wooden chest of Oriental make.

'Are the goods undamaged?' I demanded.

'Aye, milord, all in one piece, as you wanted,' the elder man said. He set down his end of the chest on the rug, as I directed, and touched his cap, respectfully. The younger fellow did the same.

'And you were unobserved?'

'Nobody saw us. Like you said, milord, we was very careful. Just looked like a pair of blokes removing an old unwanted linen chest, weren't we Bill?' The younger man nodded.

'Enough! I told you: no names to be spoken.'

'Don't worry. We never said a word, did we?' The other shook his head, remaining silent.

'And you went to the right house... this is the item I specified?'

'With red hair, like you said, milord.'

'Good. You may go. See Appleby. He will give you the sum agreed, once I have ascertained the condition of the delivery.'

As the wretches departed, I could hardly contain my excitement. The bolt was stubborn, un-oiled, but I forced it back. I opened the lid slowly, not certain how the contents would lay. She was well swaddled in a heavy, military blanket – once an officer's possession, to judge by the quality of the embroidered badge of the Coldstream Guards. The shrouded form began to wriggle and make muffled sounds of protest. With great care, I began unwrapping my new acquisition. As I unfolded the blanket a great swathe of red and copper-gold hair tumbled out, free of its pins, like a Medusa unleashed.

'Get me out of here, you devil, whoever you are!' The voice penetrated the cascade of hair as through a curtain, but there was no mistaking it sounded angry, rather than fearful.

I parted the hair, revealing a fine-boned, narrow face but the eyes were afire.

'How dare you truss me up like a Christmas goose!'

I unwound more of the blanket and suddenly her arm came free and she struck me across my face. I staggered back. Those stupid fools hadn't thought to bind her hands! I should never have entrusted others with the task.

She was out of the chest, running for the library windows. I leapt at her but succeeded only in grabbing her skirt. Cloth tore, but she wrenched herself from my grasp and kicked open the French windows. I was stunned to see my prize hitch up her skirts, sprint across the lawn and climb the old apple tree, making a lunge for the garden wall and disappearing over it. I had never seen a woman so agile, apart from acrobats at the music hall, but then I recalled my research. Nell Sutton had been a street drab, living by her wits, before she married a policeman. A new name and a respectable address could not undo the years of hardship in a few months. No doubt she had had to escape the law more often than she had shared a bed with it.

I swept a pile of books from the desk, sending them crashing to the floor. Never before had a woman – or anyone else – thwarted my intentions so utterly. Darwin's *Origin of Species* fell open on the rug. I straightened my waistcoat, finding comfort in the smoothness of silk. Mankind might have animal origins, but I had risen above such base emotions. I calmed myself with a generous whisky and soda. I needed to rethink my plans. My quarry would now be on its guard too, which would add a delicious piquancy to the dish when it was finally served. I went to the door of the library and found Appleby waiting in the corridor.

'Don't pay those inept bumbling fellows a single penny. The item is not enclosed in the chest as I demanded.'

CHAPTER 8

NELL JUMPED from the top of the wall, landing in a soft pile of fallen leaves. The fellow raking them together looked surprised but, out of habit, touched his cap to a woman – even one behaving in so unladylike a manner. Nell hurried away, fearful the gardener might be one of her abductors, though he seemed harmless.

Taking a moment to catch her breath, she paused to get her bearings. Where was this place? All around her were trees and greenery. Used to the grime and narrow, crowded ways of the city, Nell felt unnerved by such fresh, wide spaces, broad swathes of grass and open sky. She was high on a hill, but below lay her home, London, cloaked in its familiar, faint pall of sulphurous smoke. With a backward glance but seeing no sign of pursuit, she set off, down the hill, fearing any moment to see angry men behind her. Keeping to the edge of a copse of trees – a hiding place, if need be – she ran towards the city. She had little idea as to the precise whereabouts of her home in that great rambling jumble of houses and factories, churches and warehouses, but someone would surely be able to direct her.

Nell was shivering. The autumn wind was bracing and she had neither cloak nor shawl, nor a hat, and her hair hung loose as a common woman's, all dishevelled from being trussed up in that blanket. What a sight she must look. But there was no time to waste, worrying about her appearance. She must get home. Albert would be frantic if she weren't there to greet him. Imagining her husband's concern brought tears to her eyes and she scrubbed them away, turning her thoughts to her life before Albert Sutton had rescued her from the slums. Not so long ago, she had been an independent woman, relying on her ingenuity to survive from day to day. She must do that now.

Crossing a canal by means of a set of lock gates, Nell found the parkland stretched before her. To her left, she could hear strange animal sounds coming from beyond an enclosed area. She had heard such sounds once before. Albert had brought her here – unless there were other, similar places she didn't know of – to the zoo. They had spent a summer Sunday afternoon watching lions and leopards, an elephant, camels and giraffes. This was Regent's Park. But it was a huge area, bordered by grand houses and it was hard to determine her general direction as she sought a way out of the park, between the high walls of private gardens belonging to rich folk.

Marylebone was far less affluent. Although reassured to find herself surrounded by tenements and terraced houses once more, Nell was soon lost in the maze of streets and, as the sun disappeared into a blanket of cloud and chimney smoke, it proved almost impossible to know in which direction she walked. More by accident than calculation, as the houses became larger and more self-important once again, she realised she had reached Mayfair, where once she had sold flowers to the wealthy. Curzon Square had been her patch and once she was in Piccadilly, she skirted Green Park and turned left into Grosvenor Place. Passing the Royal Mews and keeping the steam and chuff and clank of Victoria Station on her right hand, Nell reached Carlisle

Place and that so-welcome sight of Summerlea Villas. After a journey that seemed like many miles, she was home.

~

At least this evening he was not greeted by the smell of his supper, burning. But neither did Nell hasten to welcome him in the hallway. Even Blackstock failed to appear, to wind himself, snakelike, around Albert's ankles, threatening to send him headlong on the hall runner.

'Nell!' No answer. So Albert took off his Norfolk jacket and Homburg hat – copying HRH's fashion, though requiring a far less generous girth. It was no easy task, what with one arm in a sling, to remove his coat and hang it on the hook, (no footman to take them from a humble inspector). He went through to the kitchen at the back of the house. His wife was slumped at the table, her face hidden by a curtain of titian hair. The cat was folded upon himself beneath her chair.

'Nell, dearest? Whatever ails you? Are you unwell?' He touched her lightly on the arm and she started, knocking his hand away. 'Nell?'

She stared at him, her eyes wide with fear, like a creature of the forest affrighted by a hunter. She flung herself at him, causing him to stagger back under her weight, though she was slender as a stair rod. He winced as she crushed his bandaged arm. The cat also sprang up and joined in the melée, darting between Albert's feet as it shot under the stone sink in the corner.

'Oh, Albert. It was so horrible... horrible. They took me and threw me in a box and I thought they would... And then I jumped over a wall and I heard the lions and...'

'Whoa, whoa, now. Steady up, Nell; you make no sense.'

'But I didn't know where I was and I had to get home to cook your dinner...'

'Sit down and I'll make us some tea. Then you can tell me everything. Did you doze off and have a bad dream?'

'The park was huge and the houses so grand... I never saw such a place and...'

He began to fill the old kettle from the little hand-pump over the shallow sink, the sudden spurts of water drowning out Nell's next words.

'What did you say?' He laughed. 'I thought you said 'kidnapped'? My ears must be deaf from that buffeting the other night.'

'Do not make a jest of this!' Nell cried, 'I *was* kidnapped by two ruffians. Scoundrels with huge hands.'

Albert left the kettle standing in the sink.

'Nell, Nell... who was it?' he demanded, holding her close, feeling her trembling against his chest. 'Did they hurt you?'

'Yes! Well, no, not really, but they scared me so, bundling me in an old smelly blanket and shoving me into that box like... like a sack of carrots. It was horrible, I tell you, so horrible, and I don't know why.' She began to sob, her tears soaking into his shirt front.

Usually Albert was perfectly capable when it came to giving comfort to victims of crime but, in this case, it was very difficult, not because he felt no compassion for Nell but because too many other emotions welled up inside him.

'When I get my hands on these devils, they'll suffer for this. I'll wring their necks like chickens; I'll beat them to a paste; I'll make them regret they were ever born. Who were they? Did you see their faces? When I catch them...' He left the sentence unfinished. Catching them? How should he go about that? It would be no easy task.

He eased Nell down into the chair by the table. A basket of clean linen sat, awaiting the application of a smoothing iron. He found a rumpled handkerchief among the shirts and chemises and held it out to her. Her hand was cold as marble as they touched. His own throat felt tight, constricted by tears he refused to shed.

'Dry your eyes, dearest,' he said, softly, 'Then you can tell me every detail of what you recall.'

As they sat over cups of sugary tea, Nell told Albert everything of her terrifying ordeal, interrupted by the occasional sniff and shudder. He did his best to take pencilled notes in his Metropolitan Police-issue notebook, writing with his left hand. As if that wasn't untidy enough, his writing became more jerky and illegible whenever his anger threatened to overwhelm him as her awful story unfolded.

'But you found your way home from that large house,' he said, turning to begin a fifth page of near-unreadable notes, 'So you could find your way back there?'

'Well, yes. But it's all such a muddle in my head, as I told you. I just ran and ran until I recognised Curzon Square, then I knew my way from there, but before that... it was open country with trees, then a maze of streets and buildings. I never stopped to look closely. I just wanted to get home, thinking I'd be safe, but I'm not safe, even here, am I? They know where I live. Oh, Albert, what if they come back?'

Nell was in his arms again, knocking aside his well-chewed pencil as the notebook tumbled off the table, pages coming loose, and all he could do was hold her tightly. He had no answer.

Not yet.

CHAPTER 9

Monday, 15ᵗʰ October
Scotland Yard

OF COURSE, no one recognised me when I limped into the police station at Scotland Yard. My tattered coat, unshaven face and broken-brimmed hat marked me out a member of the lower classes – the very sort of fellow I most despise, but the disguise was necessary today. I went to the sergeant's desk, removing my hat as a subservient member of the public should, revealing an untidy mop of greying hair, not my own.

'Name?' the sergeant enquired, glancing up from his copy of *The Police News* within which, I noted, was *The Racing Post* well circumscribed with red pencil.

'James C-Corn'ill, s-sir,' I said, seemingly stuttering in nervous anxiety, 'Though friends call me Jimmy. It's my wife, she's gawn m-missing, sir.'

'Missing, you say? You sure she's not just run off with the coalman?' the sergeant laughed at his own joke, his florid jowls flapping beneath an extensive moustache much in need of a good trimming and waxing.

'She's not runned off nowhere, sir. My Peggy's a faithful ol' duck. She wouldn't just go awf with somebody; not my Peggy.' I allowed my voice to rise in pitch. 'Something's 'appened to 'er, I knows it, sir, something 'orrible.' I took out a sizeable red cloth and wiped my eyes, pressing hard on my eyelids to force tears. I sniffed loudly. 'You gotta find 'er, sir.'

'Now, now, Mr Cornhill, I'm sure your Peggy's right as rain somewhere, safe as houses. You'll see.' The sergeant opened a black notebook and licked his pencil before printing today's date – no clerk he, he wrote 'Munday'. 'Now let me take down a few details and we'll see what's what, shall we? Name of the missing person?'

'Peggy, that is Margaret Corn'ill, Mrs.' I dabbed at my eyes again and made sobbing noises.

'Place of residence?'

'Inkerman Terrace. Number 15A. It's a shared 'ouse, sir, we rents the upstairs.' Such a place did exist – I had made sure – but the downstairs tenants at Number 15 were away (he at Her Majesty's pleasure and she at her sister's in Fulham). Number 15A upstairs had stood empty for three weeks, since the tenant, James Cornhill, lay in St Thomas's hospital, having been run down by a fine coach. Cornhill had neither wife nor family, but an anonymous relative had paid another month's rent in advance just a fortnight ago. It was money I considered well spent.

'Age and description of the missing person?'

'Thirty-seven next b-birthday, sir. My poor Peggy, w-where can she be?' I cried, edging towards an admirable fit of hysteria, tearing the red cloth in my anguish. This was a performance worthy of the best music-hall melodrama, if I say so myself.

'Now then, don't take on so, Mr Cornhill, calm

yourself. We'll find your Peggy if we have to turn London upside down, won't we, Inspector Sutton?'

To my delight, Albert Sutton himself had come out to see what the fuss was about. I had intended it should happen so, but it was a chancy thing. My plan was working well, thus far. To conceal my glee, I flung myself at Sutton, grabbing his coat, pleading with him to find the elusive Peggy. I felt him wince as I pulled on his arm, still in its sling, but I continued to sob and wail, making such a scene.

'Come into the office, Mr er...'

'James Cornhill,' the sergeant said.

'Thank you, Sergeant Hobhouse. Now, Mr Cornhill, sit down if you please.' Sutton eased me into a chair beside his cluttered desk. He hovered indecisively for a few moments, straightening the jacket I had severely disarranged, easing his arm in its sling. Clearly, it still gave him considerable discomfort – that was pleasing. 'I think we could both benefit from a nice cup of tea, don't you agree?' he said. He smiled at me, patted my shoulder.

Patronising the lower classes, I thought. I agreed: tea would be a good restorative. I blew my nose on the cloth, hiding my face which threatened to exhibit a blaze of triumph. Must keep in character.

'Constable Michaelson!' I heard Sutton call out from the doorway. 'Where are you, Michaelson? I beg your pardon, Mr Cornhill. There's no sign of my constable – never a Bobby when you need one, as they say. I'll have to go to the tea shop across the road myself. Would you like me to fetch you a cheese scone? They're very good.'

I nodded and sobbed a little more. Sutton took up his hat and fastened another button on his jacket which gaped ridiculously around his arm in the sling. He looked absurd. No matter: tea and scones would take time to order. Time enough for what I had in mind.

Fate had smiled on me as she so often did: with

Sutton's departure I was alone in the large office he shared with his fellows. I had chosen the time of my visit with care, knowing most policemen would be out and about their business of upholding law and order. Only Sutton was confined to the station by reason of his injured arm – another kindness of fate. I knew the arrangement of the office, having entered by means of the back window with its broken catch upon Friday last. It had a broken sash too – I had been fortunate not to have the window crash down upon me. Little wonder that Scotland Yard was in need of the new premises currently under construction nearby. Upon that earlier occasion, I had planned to take those items I required, only to learn that they were not kept as they should have been: in what passed for the Yard's filing cabinet. My endeavour had then been disrupted by the untimely arrival of a sergeant. Hence the need for this second visit.

I went to the cupboard in the corner – a heavy oak monstrosity that looked likely to fall through the floorboards under its own weight at any moment. Having investigated its lock and contents on my previous visit, I knew to take care not to be submerged in a torrent of foolscap manila envelopes – such was their filing system. However, this time I had no need of the pick-lock I had brought with me. Sutton hadn't bothered to lock it, even with a lowlife member of the public left alone in the room. What utter carelessness! He deserved to suffer the consequences of his gross inefficiency.

What I sought was here on this occasion. I selected the envelopes marked 'Whitechapel Incidents' in red ink and emptied the little cash box of what they called 'evidence'. The evidence seemed to consist of the ill-gotten gains of a recent robbery which the police had managed to retrieve somehow. More by luck than by good police work, I had no doubt. A bundle of pristine £5 notes in a paper band marked up as £250 and a diamond tiara looked most promising. There was also a nasty-looking knife and a set of knuckle-dusters – those I left behind.

With one final appropriation of the inspector's copy of today's *Times*, its more enticing tit-bits of information already marked up in wobbly green crayon – Sutton being right-handed and thus forced to use his left at present – I laughed to myself as I climbed out of the window, careful of the broken sash. James Cornhill disappeared into the chaotic jumble of alleyways behind Scotland Yard, his acquisitions hidden beneath his coat and an unassailable alibi, if required, from his hospital bed across the river.

The files and valuables would not be in my possession for long. Sutton's house was within walking distance and I knew precisely the place to hide them when I got there. A few days more and the inspector's fine reputation would be mired in the gutter.

This latest specimen for my collection was coming closer, tantalising me like the aroma of a fine meal served or the bouquet of vintage Bordeaux. Soon, I promised myself, soon he would be in the depths of despair and when Death offered the opportunity, he would embrace it gladly. It pleased me to muse upon which method Sutton would choose to end his miserable existence, his life without joy.

CHAPTER 10

**Wednesday, 17ᵗʰ October
Scotland Yard**

CONSTABLE MICHAELSON was sighing over the contents of the filing cupboard.

'They was here, I know. I put them on that shelf meself the other day.' He scratched his head and knelt on the dusty floorboards before a teetering heap of manila envelopes.

'What's this, constable?' Albert Sutton laughed as he stepped around the pile of paperwork and the policeman seemingly in prayer before it. 'Something awry with our devilish filing system? Surely not.'

'It's the Ripper files, sir. Inspector Abberline wants them and I can't see them in amongst this lot, but I know they was here on Saturday. Did you 'ear, sir? There's bin another leg turned up in an ostler's yard awf the Strand. A woman's. Might match wot we found by the bridge.'

'Can't be the Ripper then. That's miles out of his stamping ground.'

'Could've been the Jews though, after wot was written on the wall last time.'

Albert frowned.

'What writing was this? I read nothing about it in the reports.'

'It was at the scene of that second murder on the last day of September, in Mitre Square. Written in blood, it was, sir: somethink about the Jews not being blamed or some such. It ain't in the report 'cos Sergeant Hobhouse told me to wash it off when he saw it and not to mention it. He said we didn't want no trouble wi' the Jewish people wot live round there; people chuckin' bricks through their windders and that. Sergeant reckoned there was enough goin' on, wot with the match-girls and the dockers bein' on strike not long before and didn't want the papers gettin' hold of the story an' stirrin' things up again. That's wot he said, sir.'

'Did he, indeed? Maybe that was a wise thing, maybe not. It doesn't do to tamper with the evidence. Remember that, constable.'

'Yes, sir.'

Although he had weighty matters on his mind – not least Nell's abduction – Albert was in a better mood this morning, or he might have taken Michaelson to task over the matter. Or even Sergeant Hobhouse, come to that. But the splints had been taken off his wrist an hour ago – such blessed relief. It was badly sprained but not broken. Although still heavily bandaged, life was a deal easier now he could use his hand when needful, even if he had been instructed by the surgeon to rest it as much as he was able. And Nell's offerings of bacon and scrambled eggs for breakfast had been a veritable triumph: the eggs had barely scorched at all and the rashers were very nearly crisp at the edges. Her skills in the kitchen had decidedly improved of late.

'Knowing Mr Abberline, the files are most likely on his desk already, hidden under all the other files and reports he can never put his hand to when he needs them.' Realising he had spoken out of turn, that he should not have criticised his fellow inspector before a constable, Albert cleared his throat and hitched up his second-best trousers. 'Shall I assist you to sort the files into some semblance of order, constable?'

Both on their knees, the two men began going through the tumbled envelopes. Albert was more glad by the moment that the sling and splints had been removed from his arm.

'Ah! The Crawford case file... filed under 'J',' he muttered, 'I wondered where that had gone astray. You know, Michaelson, we really must nag *Those Upstairs* into purchasing a proper filing cabinet. This just will not do.'

'No, sir, I agree.' Michaelson took up an armful of envelopes, now restored to alphabetical order and, stretched on tip-toe, returned them to the top shelf of the cupboard. 'We'll need us another cupboard soon for this lot. Hardly no more space for the S to Z files at the bottom.'

'Well, constable, we failed to apprehend the Ripper here, I'm afraid. Not a sign of those files.' Sutton stood up, feigning a little cough to cover up the fact that his left knee cracked as he straightened up, just as it always did, embarrassing him.

'No, sir, I'll have to try to take a peek at Inspector Abberline's desk when he goes to dinner, see if it's buried there somewhere. Ain't the sort of thing to get half-inched by anybody, is it?' Michaelson grinned, a little shamefaced. 'Sorry, Mr Sutton, sir, there I was forgetting you ain't a Cockney born.'

'Fear not, constable, I'm not so lately come to these

parts that I cannot unravel a little of your rhyming slang.' He lifted down the cash-box marked EVIDENCE to clear the space and then handed Michaelson the files L to P for the right-hand end of the middle shelf.

'Perfect timing, Mr Sutton.' Sergeant Hobhouse said as he entered the office. 'I have Lord Grosvenor-Berkeley's butler at the front desk, come to collect a diamond tiara and £250 in new notes, stolen a week ago from his lordship's place in Primrose Hill. Described 'em ezzackerly, sir, so I s'pose he'll have to take them. Says his lordship won't be prosecuting the miscreant. Puts it down to carelessness in not locking it all away hisself.'

Sutton frowned.

'But the thief, Tight Jim Giles, admitted he stole them from a carriage waiting outside the Palace of Westminster. The Lord Chancellor's carriage, no less, the cheeky rogue. What has this to do with Lord Grosvenor-Berkeley, sergeant?'

'Don't know, Mr Sutton, but I'll find out when...' Sergeant Hobhouse stared into the open box before him. There was no tiara, no pristine bank notes, just a knife and a nasty-looking knuckleduster. 'Well I go to the foot of our stairs! Gawd luv us, there's nothink here, Mr Sutton: no tiara, that's for sure, and no money. Jus' Tight Jim's ironmongery, that's all.'

Sutton looked into the box too. Although there was no doubting Sergeant Hobhouse's eye-sight was more than sufficient, Albert had to see for himself that there was no mistake. Impossible as it seemed, the valuables had disappeared while in police custody.

'P'rhaps another officer is examining them as evidence, sir?' Constable Michaelson suggested helpfully, but they all knew that was not the case.

'They're gawn,' said the sergeant, his face mournful as a bloodhound's, his whiskers drooping. 'There'll be hell to pay when *Them Upstairs* learn of this.'

'Indeed there will,' Sutton sighed. 'Instigate a search of these entire premises, Sergeant Hobhouse. The items must have been mislaid. They cannot have gone too far, I'm certain.'

The sergeant's whiskers drooped even lower, if that was possible, at the prospect of trying to organise a search through the chaotic offices of the Metropolitan Police Detective Division. Worse still, the moment he set things in motion, everyone, including *Them Upstairs*, would become aware that the valuables had gone missing.

'Mr Sutton, couldn't we make a more... wots the word... circumspektif look-see around the office, just in case?'

'This is going to have to become official, sergeant.' Seeing Hobhouse's obvious reluctance, Albert sighed. 'Very well. You and Michaelson have until two o'clock this afternoon to find the tiara and the money, quietly, discreetly and without fuss. After that, I must go and admit our negligence to *Those Upstairs*. Do what you can, Hobhouse, Michaelson, I'm not relishing the prospect any more than a funeral on a foggy Monday in November. Thank you both; I know you'll do your best.'

'And we haven't found the Ripper files neither, sir,' the constable reminded him.

'No, indeed, so keep a look out for those also.'

'What shall I tell Inspector Abberlene, sir, seein' he asked for them an hour ago?'

'Blame me, constable. Tell him I'm using them at the moment. Sorry. I realise, I'm asking you to lie, but he probably has them on his desk, under the rest of the files.'

As the two men left him alone, although his thoughts were in turmoil, Albert considered it prudent to keep to his usual morning habits, to give them time to make their discreet enquiries. Seeing the clock on the wall said it was past the hour of eleven, he was late for his morning cup of tea at Kitty Mumbles' teashop. Taking up his Homburg hat and fastening his coat – so much easier now he was able to use both hands – he was about to leave the office when it suddenly occurred to him. He fished in his pocket for his keys and locked his desk drawers and the filing cupboard. After all, only the other day his copy of *The Times* had mysteriously disappeared from his desk. The horse was long since bolted, as they say, but Albert would be locking the stable doors from now on.

CHAPTER 11

Thursday, 18th October
Scotland Yard

INSPECTOR ALBERT Sutton had spent almost two hours first thing this morning with Dr Philips in the mortuary at St Thomas's. Another corpse had been washed up on the Victoria Embankment. That it was female had been supposed from the length of hair and the remains of a silk petticoat, but otherwise, it was so badly decomposed and ravaged by the denizens of the darkest waters of the Thames that it was hard to tell what the unfortunate soul had been while it lived. Dr Philips had confirmed it was a woman but more than that he couldn't say. She might have been in the river for weeks, months maybe, and there was little chance of finding out who she was or how she had met her fate. Even so, Albert had been required to attend. Now all he wanted was a nice cup of tea to wash the taste of formaldehyde out of his mouth and to fill his nostrils with the delicious aroma of a hot scone straight from the oven.

He sniffed at his sleeve, then his lapel. The stink of the mortuary still clung to his clothes. He could but hope Kitty Mumbles' other customers wouldn't notice as he pushed open the door of the tea shop, setting the little brass bell tinkling. Nell could give his jacket a good airing tomorrow and a generous dose of lavender water – or perhaps not the latter; he didn't want to smell like a flower girl.

'Good morning, Mr Sutton, sir.' Kitty Mumbles hurried out from her tiny kitchen behind the counter, wiping her plump little hands on her spotless apron. 'What can I get you, sir? The usual: toast and marmalade?'

'A pot of tea, please, Kitty, and one – no, make that two – of your wonderful cheese scones, just for a change.'

'Very well, sir.' She disappeared back into her Aladdin's cave from which so many culinary delights emerged with such gratifying efficiency, it was quite miraculous.

Albert took his usual seat by the chintz-draped window, welcoming the comfort of the cushion – he had spent too long, leaning over the cold mortuary slab or else he was getting old. Thirty-six years old next month. No, he was in the prime of life, surely. Too many damp foggy nights spent poking around the river mud, that's what it was.

He turned to the newspaper he'd bought from the vendor beside Westminster Bridge, leafing through the broadsheet. It seemed *The Times* regarded yesterday's offerings from the stable in the Strand and the Thames as insufficiently news-worthy. There was no mention of the latest occupants of Dr Philips' cold table, but one or two entries in the 'lost and found' column received the attention of Albert's green-crayon for future reference.

'Here we are, sir: tea and cheese scones. Now mind you don't drip the melted butter down your jacket. And how's the arm, if you'll pardon my asking, sir?'

Albert smiled.

'Kitty, you're not old enough to be my mother, nor are you my wife, nor my laundress. But as for my arm: it is mending nicely, thanks to your prompt ministrations after my mishap.'

'Oh, sir, but I was just saying because it's a decent coat, even if it does tell me you've been at that 'ospital over the bridge again.'

'It smells that bad?'

'I have a special sensitive nose is all, sir, but... all the same, sir...' Kitty Mumbles screwed up her face. 'I've got a bottle of *eau-de-cologne* in the kitchen, somewhere.'

Albert deftly cut the first scone in two and smeared each half with a generous helping of butter. Delicious. He licked his lips and brushed a stray crumb from his waistcoat before devouring the other half. He was mulling over Mrs Mumbles's suggestion, wondering whether it was more professional to smell like a long-dead corpse or Harrods' perfumery counter, when the tea shop bell tinkled and Constable Michaelson rushed in.

'Begging pardon, Mr Sutton, sir...' A wistful expression flitted across the young man's face as his eye was taken by the one scone remaining, oozing butter on the plate. 'Er, sorry to interrupt your breakfast, sir, but *Them Upstair*s have sent for you sir. Urgent, they say.'

'Isn't that always the case with them?' Albert sighed. 'What do they want?'

'Didn't say, sir, 'ceptin' you're to come at once.'

Albert drained his teacup. The second one in the pot would have to go to waste but not the remaining cheese scone. He folded up his newspaper, put on his Homburg and took a few coins from his pocket which he left on the lace tablecloth.

'Help yourself, constable,' he said, offering Michaelson the plate. 'Careful you don't drip butter on your uniform.'

~

As Albert reached the head of the stair, on his way to Chief Constable Williamson's office, the man himself came out of the door, his arm around the heaving shoulders of a weeping woman. She was well dressed in a fashionable style, carrying a little dog.

'But Dolly, we haven't seen Thomas for weeks now. You must report him as missing, I insist.' The woman mopped her eyes.

'I know, Agnes, but the lad is over twenty-one, a grown man, and he's always had a bit of a wild streak about him. You know that,' the Chief Constable tried to console her.

'But suppose some grave misfortune has befallen him. I'll never forgive myself, Dolly.' The little animal yapped as she held him too tightly and struggled free, leaping from her arms.

'Sutton, get that dog,' Williamson ordered. 'Don't worry, dear, the boy will come home when he runs out of money, as he always does. Now, the sergeant will make you a nice cup of tea. I have business to attend to. Good day, Agnes.' The Chief Constable almost snatched the puffball of fluff that Albert had caught and returned it to its owner.

'Come in, Sutton. Close the door,' he said. Both men brushed dog hairs from their jackets.

'Trouble, sir? Anything I can do to help?' Albert offered.

'Nephew's gone off somewhere. Not the first time. But that's neither here nor there. Private matter.' Williamson cleared his throat noisily as he sat behind the desk and began stroking his thick beard. He cleared his throat again.

Albert stood before Chief Constable Adolphus Williamson, hat in hand, utterly baffled by the summons.

'Well, inspector,' Williamson said at last, 'What do you have to say about this, eh? Some explanation is called for, don't you think?'

On the mahogany desk between them lay a rectangular package, wrapped in sacking and tied with twine, the sort Nell used to use to bind her little flower posies. There was also what appeared to be a sheet of screwed up newspaper.

'I don't know, sir. What are we talking about?'

'These, of course.' Williamson nudged the packages with the riding crop he always kept to hand, moving them both an inch closer to Albert. 'Recognise them, do you?'

'No, sir, I've never seen them before.'

'Sure of that?'

'Positive, sir.'

Williamson leaned back in his chair, the wooden joints creaking as they bore the Chief Constable's considerable bulk.

'Constable Thompson!' Williamson bellowed towards the door.

A middle-aged constable, quite unknown to Albert, scurried in. His uniform was impeccably neat as he – Albert could hardly credit it – made a little bow to the man behind the desk. 'Tell the inspector where you found the packages.'

'Certainly, Chief Constable Williamson, sir.' Thompson gave a little cough and stood at attention, his eyes focused straight ahead as though the words were written on the wall behind his senior officer. 'You instructed me, sir, first thing this morning, at seven of the clock precisely, following an anonymous tip-off, to attend at the address of one Lysander Albert Dalrimple Sutton at Number Six Summerlea Villas, Carlisle Place, close to the Victoria Railway Station.'

'What!' Albert cried, 'What were you...'

'Silence, Sutton,' Williamson warned, 'Your turn will come. Continue Thompson.'

The constable coughed again:

'I proceeded to the back garden plot of the aforesaid

dwelling, Number Six Summerlea Villas, whereupon I made an examination of the potting shed...'

Albert squirmed beneath Williamson's unwavering stare. A multitude of questions flew inside his head, battering his brain, but two were most prominent for now – what about Nell and how had the devils found out his full name, names he never, ever used, names he was certain had been his parents' private joke upon him and the vicar at his christening. Now everyone would share the joke. He'd never live it down.

'In the aforementioned potting shed...' Thompson was saying, gazing fixedly at the wall behind Williamson's head, stiff as a guardsman on duty at Buckingham Palace, '...I came upon a hessian-wrapped package, sir, nefariously concealed behind a pile of seed trays. I took possession of the said package and a second, smaller package, wrapped in newspaper – a page from *The Times*, to be precise, dated Monday last – that was likewise concealed in an otherwise empty four-inch earthenware plant pot, labelled *Lilium regalis*. That's what it said, sir. I then conveyed the aforesaid packages to you, sir, as per your instructions.'

'Very well, Thompson, you may go.'

Thompson gave another little bow, seeming on the verge of tugging his forelock like a tradesman.

'Very good, sir. Thank you, sir. At your service, Chief Constable, sir.'

'Get out!'

'Yes, sir, thank you.' The constable bowed again and retreated backwards to the door, like a royal courtier leaving the presence of his monarch.

Williamson blinked and shook his head. Sycophancy annoyed him, but Thompson had his uses.

'Well? What have you to say now, Sutton?'

'Nothing, sir. I have no knowledge of either package or their contents.' Albert spoke clearly, defying any trace of a tremor in his voice, but his insides were in turmoil. He had the feeling something awful was about to happen here.

'We will determine later how these items came to be secreted on your premises, but for now, so there can be no misunderstanding of the subject under discussion, you will open the packages.'

Albert obeyed. The twine had already been unknotted and he simply folded back the layers of sacking to reveal a bundle of foolscap paper, tied with string. On the top was a manila envelope, empty now but headed 'Case nos. 159A/159D – Whitechapel Incidents aka The Ripper Case', the words underlined twice. Albert swallowed hard. His hands were shaking as he slowly removed the newspaper that wrapped the second package. He had noticed that two columns of type had been marked up with green crayon. He knew now what he would find inside. There before him lay a diamond tiara and a sheaf of unused £5 notes still in their paper band.

He could feel his career – his whole world – was about to fall apart.

CHAPTER *12*

Friday, 19th October
St John's Club, Mayfair

S O, MY plans are taking shape at last; the fiasco of
the failed abduction of Sutton's wife need not make
any difference now. Appleby tells me that the word
is on the street that a senior detective – as yet unnamed, of
course – is guilty of the most heinous acts of misconduct,
thievery being the least of them, misappropriating evidence,
tampering with official reports, etc. etc. Oh, how I wish I
might have been there, a fly upon the wall, to have observed
Sutton in his moment of realisation. I would like to have
made notes for my records of this, my latest and most
ambitious experiment.

I shall dine at my club tonight. The senior members
of Her Majesty's Metropolitan Constabulary are certain to
be there as usual and with so much to discuss, it should be
a most informative evening.

The private dining room was abnormally quiet when

I arrived promptly at eight o'clock that evening. No sign of Chief Constable Williamson nor Assistant Commissioner Robert Anderson who were usually there a little before me, indulging in their second round of brandy and sodas – but not tonight it appeared. Perhaps new developments in the Sutton case had kept them at their desks until a later hour than was their custom.

'Bring me a brandy and I'll have the roast pork tonight for a change.'

'Certainly, my lord, and here is the theatre ticket for tomorrow night, as you requested.' He passed me a white envelope upon which was scrawled *Lord Grosvenor-Berkeley, The Lyceum Theatre* in a barely legible hand. 'I regret, sir, that your usual box was already taken but, at such short notice, I was able to get you a seat in the club's private box. I'm afraid the Honourable Ignatius Swinbury has also booked four seats in the same box.'

'But that is most inconvenient.'

'It is a very popular performance, sir. It was fortunate that any tickets were left at all and it is rumoured that the Prince of Wales himself has taken your most favoured box.'

'Yes, yes, very well. Charge the ticket to my account, as usual.'

The butler bowed and slipped silently away. I do so dislike the way the fellow slithers through doorways and comes upon one noiselessly; it is disconcerting indeed to discover him lurking at one's shoulder without any warning of his approach. If I should decide at some point to add him to my collection, it will be by some means that shall cause him to make a considerable outcry and thus give me much personal satisfaction. But he does have his uses.

When the butler brought my brandy, I pointed out to him that one of the gas lamps was flickering and to attend to it directly. Its uncertain light was annoying me as I attempted to read Mr Stevenson's recent novella: *The*

Strange Case of Dr Jekyll and Mr Hyde – a most amusing tale which is being performed on stage to great acclaim – hence my theatre visit tomorrow evening. A little light-hearted diversion will be welcome indeed.

Dinner was disappointing: the pork was stringy, the gravy cold and the roast potatoes and cabbage a grey, soggy, indeterminate mess. I berated the butler soundly, calling him an idle bounder of such temerity to have dared serve me this miserable fare. I demanded that the cook be summoned forthwith from the kitchen to account for his failings. While I waited, I noticed the Assistant Commissioner and the Chief Constable were now seated at a table by the door, consuming generous helpings of the pork. Their platters steamed, giving off the rich aromas of the meat in its thick, dark gravy. I heard their knives cutting into the crisp roast potatoes; saw the delicate green shreds of cabbage heaped beside. How different from that which they had dared set before me! Heads would roll for this. Later. For now, the conversation from the policemen's table attracted my notice. The senior officers were becoming over loud and, normally, I would have demanded they desist at once, but the subject matter was clearly relevant to my present object of study.

'I will not credit it, Dolly,' Assistant Commissioner Anderson was saying, waving a forkful of cabbage, 'I recommended his promotion to the rank of inspector personally. Albert Sutton's record is impeccable. He cannot be guilty.'

'The evidence is plain enough, Robin. The Ripper files and the missing valuables were found at his home.' Williamson stroked his beard pensively. 'I like it no more than you, but the man's gone rogue on us, Robin, and that's the unpalatable truth.'

'But it's just circumstantial. Anyone could have planted the evidence in his garden shed.'

'But why would they do it? What motive would anyone have to concoct false charges against the man?'

'He's a policeman, Dolly, and a damn good one. At some point in his career, he's bound to have put away some felon or other whose relatives might want to take revenge upon him.' Anderson finished his brandy and soda and chinked the empty glass with his knife to attract the butler's attention for another drink. 'And that's your motive, no doubt.'

I smiled to myself. How deluded were the Metropolitan Police in thinking there always had to be a logical explanation? A reason; a motive for every crime. As though pleasure could not be a motive in itself.

'Then why take and hide the Ripper files, eh? Explain that. I can think of only one reason, Robin, much as I shudder at the ramifications: that there is something in them which implicates Sutton in those dreadful crimes. Could he know the identity of the Ripper? Is it a friend or family member? Is it even possible that Sutton himself is the Ripper?'

'That's ridiculous, Dolly, and you know it. Sutton is as straight a rod as you may find.'

'Are you sure of that? Look at the girl he wed last spring. Hardly a daughter of decent up-standing parentage, is she now? Straight from Shepherd's Market, so I heard.'

'The man has a soft heart.'

'A soft head, more like. She could be leading him astray. Who can say what low-lifes she may be acquainted with? I tell you, Robin, my nose is twitching over this business and I don't like the smell of it one bit.'

'It's just the boiled cabbage, Dolly, believe me,' Anderson tried to make a jest of it, but I could see the Chief Constable had grave doubts about Sutton and even the Assistant Commissioner was becoming uneasy.

~

Later, I took the management at St John's to task concerning their poor service and a complementary double brandy did nought to soothe me nor compensate me for such an insult as had been perpetrated. I demanded that both the butler and the cook be dismissed immediately without references and, as one of the club's most influential and distinguished members of long-standing, I expected those demands to be carried out right away. If they were not, I threatened to withdraw my membership; the management would wish to avoid such ignominy at all cost, so I will be expecting better service – and a new butler – in future.

Saturday, 20th October

The following evening, I attended the performance of *Dr Jekyll and Mr Hyde* which cheered me enormously. *The Lyceum Theatre* was crowded and smoky, but the limelight was used effectively. The actor who played the dual roles, one Richard Mansfield, was quite adept at the transformation from Hyde to Jekyll. I observed him with a keen eye, noting how the change from monster to man was achieved solely by an alteration of attitude and nothing of disguise – a quite remarkable achievement. An amusing incident occurred in the box I was forced to share when Ignatius Swinbury – known to me as a member at my club – swooned at the sight of one of the more imaginative 'deaths' on stage. What a pathetic specimen of manhood, I thought; after all, the 'victim' was merely acting a part. I wondered how the insipid fellow would behave if a real murder was enacted before his eyes.

I returned to the club for a night-cap and was much gratified to see that the butler was a new man although he took the liberty of introducing himself – Shedman or Statham or some such – as if it mattered. Of course, his lack of foreknowledge entailed the giving of my name by the doorman and necessitated my ordering my preferred reserve brandy. The fellow even enquired as to whether I would want soda with it, but my withering look was sufficient to inform him that the best Armagnac would not suffer such mindless adulteration.

He served my drink with sufficient discretion without being overly obsequious. His left shoe squeaked a little as he walked – at least I would no longer suffer the intrusion of any sudden, unheralded appearances. The Honourable Ignatius Swinbury was there in the library, being revived by his friends with copious amounts of cheap medicinal brandy and cold compresses. I was hard put not to laugh aloud, knowing the cause of his indisposition. When I enquired of the butler why the foolish fellow was cluttering up the library, I was informed that a bedchamber was being prepared for him and a physician had been sent for. An unnecessary fuss. I would have thrown him out into the street and let the chill night air revive him.

Less than an hour later, as I was sipping my third brandy and deciding whether to order a bed for the night or send for my brougham, the butler came in, laden with lengths of black crepe.

'Please excuse the intrusion, my lord,' he murmured, bowing, 'I have been instructed to drape the mirrors and mantles with mourning bands, sir, on account of the death of a member upon the premises.'

'Who has died?' My interest was roused.

'The Honourable Ignatius Swinbury died a half hour since of a surfeit, so they say.'

A surfeit! Is that what they call it? Died of fright more likely, I thought, the ridiculous fellow. Nevertheless, I was disappointed to have missed the opportunity of observing his passing at first hand.

CHAPTER 13

Monday, 22nd October

ALBERT WALKED the streets, oblivious as to where his feet might carry him, quite unaware of the gloomy mist gathering – the herald of another London Particular.

Suspended! And worse: without pay! The images of the morning's second encounter with Chief Constable Williamson played over and over in his mind like a never-ending magic lantern show, each glass slide more devastating than its predecessor. The endlessly repeated questions about the Ripper case notes, the money, the jewellery: questions he couldn't answer. How had they come to be in his potting shed?

He found himself in a small public garden. He didn't recognise the place but the ornate wrought iron gateway and railings, the green painted benches, the orderly row of plane trees and flowerbeds were typical of the little oases of verdant relief from the city's grime, donated by some wealthy imperialist or another to the benefit of lesser mortals. On a fine day it probably looked delightful, but now the chill of autumn and the insidious fog drained the last few dregs of colour from the falling leaves, the frost-burned spikes of hollyhocks and shrivelled dahlias.

Albert's thoughts were no less bleak. Williamson had demanded his warrant card and the keys to his desk. Even his treasured police whistle, kept since his days as a lowly constable on the beat. He felt somehow naked without the firm leather wallet tucked into the inside pocket of his jacket, the authoritative jingle of keys in his coat and, worst of all, desperately isolated and vulnerable, knowing he could no longer summon the assistance of his fellows without the whistle. Now he only had the key to his house and for how much longer could he retain hold of that?

He sat on a fog-wet bench and huddled deeper into his coat. The rent was paid for this month but beyond that... He and Nell were always prudent, but now they could be penniless and homeless in a few weeks. He closed his eyes and felt a suspicious stinging-salt sensation. A lump lodged in his throat which he couldn't swallow away. Pull yourself together, Sutton, he told himself, but it was the thought of having to tell Nell that unmanned him. The better life he had promised her when they were wed, telling her she would never go hungry again, never have to spend another night on the street. Would she find that these recent months of comfort were nothing but a brief respite? That his promises meant nothing?

He sat there, rehearsing speeches in his head, how to break the news to her gently. But he couldn't get the words right. How could he crush all her hopes for the future in a single sentence? He couldn't do it. He got up from the bench and walked. Where didn't matter: just one foot in front of the other as the thickening fog wrapped itself around him like a clammy discoloured shroud.

As he left the little garden, he could have sworn he

heard laughter. Not the laughter of friends sharing a jest or lovers happy to be together or youngsters playing. No. If the sound was not just there in his imagination, then he knew, somehow, it was laughter at his expense, but when he looked around there was nothing but a swirl of grubby mist between the dark blurs of the plane trees.

~

Inspector Albert Sutton's transformation was even more incredible than that I had witnessed at *The Lyceum* upon Saturday last, when Mansfield turned from the monstrous Mr Hyde back into the respectable Dr Jekyll. But this was no actor's sham. In the space of barely more than an hour, I had observed Sutton leaving home, walking tall and confident, striding into Scotland Yard as a man well respected by all, so certain of himself; yet he had left the building like a whipped dog, cowering and cringing, fearing another beating.

I followed him in his heedless perambulations, watching as the realisation of his situation piled its cumbersome burden onto his shoulders, heavier and weightier with every step he took. His abject misery was a wonder to behold; my experiment a success beyond expectation. My only fear was – seeing him blunder across various thoroughfares, blind to any vehicles hastening past – that he might be slain by accident, instead of taking his own life, as I intended he should.

By a most circuitous route, he entered Hyde Park. It was becoming increasingly difficult to follow him. For minutes at a time, I would lose him in the thickening fog, but I was determined. I caught up with him again as he came to stand beside the Serpentine. He stood there, staring into its dull waters for so long, I began to think my experiment was about to reach its climax far too soon. How disappointed I should be to see it end so precipitously. The thought crossed my mind that, if Sutton did jump in, mayhap I should play the Good Samaritan and drag him out? How amusingly ironic that would be; that the sole engineer of his despair should save him. But of course, it would simply be the means of denying him the relief he sought; a means of prolonging his misery. It would also make the other little incidents I had arranged to increase his woes superfluous and exceedingly disappointing.

Even I was chilled to the bone, waiting while he made his decision. An unnatural early twilight had fallen because of the fog and I was tempted by thoughts of a severely belated luncheon at my club, but I could not cease my observations at such a crucial point. Sutton took a half pace forward. The toes of his shoes overlapped the water's edge by a hair's breadth. Standing but a few yards from him, his face was unclear to me, but I was certain his lips moved, perhaps in a final act of prayer before the deed. Quite unaware of my presence, he removed his Homburg and flung it before him, out into the lake. It disappeared into the vaporous, ghostly curtain that hung above the water like theatrical drapes, about to part and reveal the denouement, the final act of the show to me, the rapt audience.

~

Afterwards, Albert couldn't remember quite why he had thrown his perfectly good hat into the Serpentine. He wasn't even sure how he came to be there in the deserted park on such a filthy afternoon. But the hat had disturbed a flotilla of ducks, floating unseen in the mist. They set up such a quacking and squawking and a fountain of spray as they burst skywards, Albert was shaken from his mindless reverie. He discovered his feet, lapped by the Serpentine's icy waters, were numb, as were his fingers and his teeth chattered. He had to get home before he caught his death of cold, no matter that it meant facing Nell, telling her the dreadful news.

~

At home in Summerlea Villas, Nell was wondering where Albert could be. For once, she was pleased that the fried liver and onions for his dinner were neither underdone nor burnt to a cinder, but they would spoil if she had to reheat them. The rhubarb crumble had also turned out well. Perhaps she was getting used to the range at last. Blacking it to perfection every morning since their marriage had not yet been matched by the dishes that came out of it but she was improving – gradually – and was by no means ashamed of the meal she would present to Albert this time. When he arrived home.

Just then, there was a knock at the front door. If Albert had forgotten his key, he knew well enough that the backdoor would be unlocked. Straightening her apron, Nell went down the hallway.

'Who is it?' she called out since no visitors were expected.

'Maudie Cooper!'

The name meant nothing to Nell. Puzzled, she opened the door to be confronted by a woman of middle age, her lips and cheeks crimson with rouge and the tattered grubby lace of her petticoat showing beneath a shabby skirt. She smiled, showing blackened teeth.

'Is Bertie 'ere?' she asked, her sour breath forcing Nell to take a step back. 'On'y he told me t' meet him on the corner, but he ain't showed up.'

'Bertie? There's no Bertie here,' Nell said. 'You've got the wrong house.'

'This is Bertie Sutton's place, ain't it? Well, you tell him he can't waste my time like this. 'Alf a crown he owes me. I could've earned that whilst I was waitin' fer him.'

'I don't know what you mean.' Nell had no idea what to do.

'Come on. Pay up, or it'll be the worse fer Bertie,' the woman insisted, holding out her hand.

Having no intention of paying the woman a penny, Nell slammed the door shut in her face. Being so ill-mannered was not her way, but she was afraid of strangers coming to the house after recent events. With the door both locked and bolted, she sighed with relief. But who was this Bertie fellow? Not Albert, surely? And yet the woman had said 'Sutton'. What was going on? Ah, yes, no doubt the woman was one of Albert's police 'informers'. That must be it. In which case, why hadn't she asked for Inspector Sutton?

CHAPTER 14

ALBERT ARRIVED home, his mind in turmoil as he considered every possible way of breaking the news to Nell of his suspension from duty and loss of pay. Be nice to her, butter her up a bit first before firing the cannon shell? Or tell her straight; get it over and done with? He still hadn't decided which as he trudged up the front steps and searched his pockets for the door key.

Of a sudden, he didn't need to bother as the door was flung open before him and Nell, all unkempt, threw herself at him, hugging his neck.

'Oh, Albert! I'm so relieved you're home. You can help me search for Blackstock. He's been gone all day; missed his dinner, which just isn't like him. If he's gone under a cartwheel or...'

Blackstock? His thoughts were so a-swirl with his own problems, it took Albert a moment or two to register that she was referring to her beloved cat.

'Nell, dearest, now calm yourself. You know that animal can take care of himself, as street-wise as any urchin in the parish. He'll have come to no harm. Probably found himself some pretty tabby paramour to serenade and forgot all about his dinner.' Albert held her close as he

88

guided her into the hallway and shut the door on the fog-shrouded street.

'I've been calling and calling him. He always comes...'

'The fog will have muffled your calls, so perhaps he didn't hear.'

'Blackstock can hear the sound of me smearing dripping on a slice of bread from the end of the terrace. He would have heard me, I know he would. And where's your hat?'

'Hat? Oh, I lost it. The wind blew...'

'But there is no wind, Albert, only a thick fog, as you pointed out.'

'Does it matter? It's gone.'

'No, I suppose we can buy you a new one.'

'No!' He snapped, then breathed in and out, slow and deep, calming himself. 'I'm sorry, Nell. I didn't mean to shout at you. When did you last see the cat?'

He put the kettle on the range, noting the liver and onions gone cold and dry in the pan, the charred topping of a fruit crumble. No supper tonight then and they couldn't afford another meal out, not now. He opened the larder, found three eggs and a bowl of dripping. No doubt this was tomorrow's breakfast but would have to serve.

'I can make us an omelette,' he said, 'In my bachelor days it was my best dish when friends came round. Do we have any cheese?'

'How can you think of food, Albert Sutton, when an innocent creature is lying helpless and in pain in a gutter somewhere?'

'Nell, you have no evidence whatever that the cat has been injured nor have I ever known an animal less helpless than that great overfed tom of yours. He eats better than I do.'

'That's not true!' Nell flounced out of the kitchen. With a sigh, Albert followed her back into the hallway. He leaned on the door jamb, arms folded, and watched his wife.

'What are you doing?'

'What does it look like?' She was pulling on her coat, fastening the buttons all wrong. 'I'm going to find Blackstock, with or without your help.'

'You won't find him in this fog: it's getting thicker by the minute.'

'I don't care. I have to try.'

'He'll be safe under cover somewhere and you'll get yourself lost.'

'I won't. I know my way around London, even in the fog. I did well enough finding my way home from that-that horrible place the other day, didn't I?'

'This isn't your old haunts, Nell. You go beyond Victoria Station, you'll be like David Livingstone in Darkest Africa.' But Albert was wasting his breath as the front door slammed behind her. She hadn't even put on her hat or gloves. Weary beyond words, he too put his coat on, still damp from his earlier traipsing through the mist, reached for his Homburg but remembered it was gone into the Serpentine and prepared to follow Nell. As soon as he opened the door on the densest of London Particulars he knew it was an impossible task. She had already disappeared but, like her, he had to try.

~

Cats. They are too much like policemen. They pursue vermin from the streets only to have them proliferate in darkness and squalor and, in the process, taint themselves with such obnoxious filth as to be regarded by respectable society as beneath acknowledgement. But I was being forced to acknowledge this particularly contemptible feline. I endeavoured to shoo it away from my place of concealment, but it did no more than arch its back higher, extrude its fur as one receiving galvanic treatment for some hideous psychological aberration and hiss at me in the manner of a locomotive departing King's Cross.

Realising there was little reason for fearing discovery now, what with the fog and increasing lack of visibility as night fell, I attempted to extricate myself from the narrow confines between the back wall and the potting shed in the Suttons' meagre excuse for a garden. I had planned to listen at the window, to observe my specimen pour out his despair to his slut of a wife and, hopefully, to hear her confront him, concerning the visit of a harlot claiming to know him. Just one of the ingenious little incidents I had planned to increase his distress further. However, the wretched cat was determined to remain sentinel, barring my passage. As soon as I caught it, it would suffer for causing me such inconvenience and discomfiture.

Warily, making endearing clucking noises, I inched towards it, extending my hand as though it held some tempting titbit. The beast stood its ground, tail waving ominously, ears flattened, unblinking eyes staring straight at me. I had not come armed, but every man has one weapon to hand so I unfastened my fly and urinated copiously on the cat, forcing it to retreat with a yowl. But it did not go far and watched as I buttoned up once more. In a sudden blur of wet fur, it sprang. I felt razor-sharp claws score my face, catching the outer corner of my left eye. Involuntarily, I cried out in pain – an instinctive reaction I never succumbed to until that moment. Putting my hands to my cheeks, both came away bloodied. The sight of my left eye was impaired by welling gore, but I could see sufficient to know my nemesis had not fled, as I would have expected.

The cat sat just a few feet away, upright, its forepaws precisely aligned, only the twitching tail, curled like a question mark on the wet grass, marring the symmetry of the pose. I had seen the like in the British Museum, in the Egyptian Gallery, amid sarcophagi and various mummified forms. The beast would soon be joining its ancient forebears but without the consolation of eternal preservation or carefully labelled public display. But its gaze did not waver from me – a disdainful glare I refused to tolerate. How dare this infernal example of *Felis domesticus* presume to get the better of me: Nathaniel Grosvenor-Berkeley!

I should have brought my pistol.

CHAPTER 15

Later that Monday evening

I **RETIRED** to my club, in no mood to explain my appearance to the likes of the new butler there. It was none of his concern to question me when I ordered him to bring hot water, clean linen and a double Armagnac to my private room, yet his raised eyebrows when he saw the blood on my face were an unspoken interrogation – of all the impudence! His left shoe still squeaked, as before. I had thought that this would be a matter of convenience to me, since the fellow could never arrive without warning, as he predecessor was wont to do. But now I was beginning to find that little rodent-like squeak most irritating.

'Do something about your shoe, Stockman! It is irksome indeed,' I told him when he brought my brandy up to my room. A footman came in behind him, carrying a pitcher of hot water, towels and bandages, and stood in the midst of the carpet. 'Put them on the wash-stand, you imbecile, then go.'

'Forgive me, my lord,' the butler said, 'But I can do nothing to rectify the matter, I fear. It is not my shoe...'

'I don't care whose it is; you are wearing it. Get a new pair.'

'It isn't the footwear, my lord, but my false leg that creaks... lost it in the Indian Mutiny, you see.'

'What is that to me? I will not tolerate your insubordinate tone, either. Get out of my

sight, Sheepman.'

'It's Stedman, my lord. My name is 'Stedman'.'

'I don't care if it's Jack the Ripper: get out!'

The looking glass above the wash-stand reflected a sorry image. That wretched feline had lacerated my face to a quite appalling degree. Mayhap, I should require the services of a surgeon to suture the deeper wounds. But I was almost smiling as I bathed away the blood: 'Jack the Ripper'! What an amusing caper that was. 'Jack' had slain his last victim, Lizzie Longstride on the 30th September. That was three weeks ago now, yet the police had as little idea as to the identity of the culprit as ever. I still had 'Jack's' watch in my possession, inscribed *To Thomas on your coming of age, from Uncle Dolly*. How many men could there be in London who bore the ridiculous soubriquet of 'Uncle Dolly'? None other than Chief Constable Adolphus Williamson: the very man who deemed Albert Sutton a possible candidate for 'Jack' when it was, in fact, his own nephew, long since diced and minced and sold by the pound by a Whitechapel butcher. I hear his sausages are most popular. How delicious was that?

The water in the porcelain bowl was stained red; the towel was bloody, but the bleeding had almost stopped. Some of Appleby's healing ointment would probably suffice, but the injuries would be impossible to disguise for weeks to come. It was a most inopportune occurrence and inconvenient.

The same evening
6, Summerlea Villas

'There you are, Blackstock! Where have you been? I've been looking everywhere.'

When Nell and Albert returned from their fruitless search of the fog-bound neighbourhood, Blackstock was washing his paws on the back doorstep. A moment before, Nell had been in tears, but the sight of the cat had her smiling as she both hugged and scolded the animal.

'You naughty little puss. Albert was so worried about you; he was quite put out. Oh, you bad, wicked darling.' Nell had the cat in her arms as Albert opened the back door. The warmth of the kitchen was welcoming after the damp chill outside, for he had given Nell his scarf and gloves to wear as they wandered the streets, calling and calling the cat.

Albert lit the gas mantles so they could see what they were doing. He had most definitely *not* been worried about the cat, only concerned for Nell. Now he would have willingly strangled the wretched creature which was being fussed and petted by his wife. He shook his head in despair as eggs and dripping – his supper – was given to the hungry cat which scoffed it down in short order. Tea. At least he could have a well-deserved cuppa. As he took the milk jug from the larder, Nell seized it.

'Poor Blackstock. He must be so thirsty.'

Albert watched the last dribble of milk being poured into the damned cat's saucer.

'That's enough, Nell! I'm entitled to be fed and watered too.'

'You can fend for yourself, you great lump; Blackstock cannot.' With that, Nell took up a large potato from the vegetable rack and hurled it at Albert, catching his shoulder.

'Take that, you unfeeling brute.' Another potato thumped him in the chest, hard. Unfortunately, she had a strong arm. Albert caught her by the wrist as she picked up a swede turnip.

'Behave like a lady, or I'll arrest you for assaulting a police officer.' Their eyes met. Nell dropped the vegetable back into the rack.

'I'm so sorry.'

Albert leaned close to kiss her cheek.

'Nell? Nell, there is blood on my scarf...'

'What? Well, I'm not hurt. Oh, no, it must be Blackstock's!' Nell was on her knees, inspecting every hair of the cat. 'His paw... both paws are bloody. Albert, he's hurt.'

Albert picked the cat up and put him on the table.

'Careful. You'll hurt him even more.'

Ignoring Nell's worries, he moved the animal so the gaslight illuminated its front paws. The left was certainly bloody and when he wiped the fur, claws and pad with a wet cloth, he discovered the cat's claw was torn. Other than that, there were no worse injuries. Nell stood wringing her hands.

'Blackstock's claw is torn. That's all, so do not fuss, Nell. It will mend. I expect he confronted a rat, maybe, or another tomcat.'

Nell came closer.

'Neither of those. Look.' With great care, she untangled a hair from between the cat's claws. Too long for a cat or rat, it was greased and shiny. 'Only men use Macassar hair oil,' she said.

Albert fetched a magnifying glass from the dresser drawer to examine the strand of dark hair they had disentangled from Blackstock's claws. Nell was trying to placate the cat with the last smear of mutton dripping, but he still managed to look quite affronted at his recent treatment: having his toes spread and tweezers used to remove the wiry human hair while he yowled at the indignity.

Albert turned the gas lamp up a little and adjusted the shade to illuminate the kitchen table as much as possible as he peered through the glass.

'Such long hair for a man,' he observed, smoothing it out on a sheet of white writing paper. It left a greasy line before springing back into curls. 'Could it simply belong to a woman who hasn't washed her hair for a long while?'

Nell gave Blackstock a settling stroke along the length of his back before coming to the table. She picked up the paper and sniffed it gently. She had an excellent sense of smell after a lifetime working with flowers.

'It's faint but definitely Macassar oil.'

'Do you know of any woman who uses it?'

'Certainly not, Albert. What kind of woman would put men's perfumed oil on their hair, I ask you? Though you might know one: Maudie Cooper? Came to the door earlier, asking for 'Bertie' who now owes her half a crown. What have you been up to, Albert? She was a loose woman if ever I saw one.'

Albert shrugged.

'I don't know. Never heard of her. She must have got the wrong address.'

'She asked for Bertie Sutton. Are you sure you don't know her?'

Albert didn't like the expression on Nell's face. What was she thinking behind those beautiful eyes?

'Positive.' He coughed, cleared his throat and returned his attention to the long hair. Having removed the grease, it was now clear that the hair wasn't so dark in colour as he had first thought: rather it was what the music hall enthusiasts at Scotland Yard liked to call 'floozy red'. Apparently, girls on the stage often dyed their hair with henna; it looked striking in the limelight. 'Could it be henna-dyed, I wonder?'

Nell took the magnifying glass from him to look for herself.

'No, not dyed. The colour goes right to the root, see? It's a man's hair. No doubt about it. And one who has been well scratched by Blackstock. With long red curls and a scratched face, he shouldn't be so hard to find.'

'And why would we want to find this distinctive looking individual, anyway?' Albert asked, sipping his now-cold, milkless tea which had sat forgotten at his elbow. 'I don't know how you can be so certain it's a man, Nell.'

She pulled out the other kitchen chair, its feet scraping the flagstone floor, making Albert wince over his last mouthful of tea as she sat opposite him. The light threw her features into shadow and he saw the underfed waif again, standing beneath a street light, offering him a posy of sweet violets: the girl he had fallen in love with. He covered her hand with his own, sensing she had something to say. Something important.

'Because I know him, Albert.'

'What! Who?'

'I don't know his name but the man who had me kidnapped and bundled into that horrid chest.' She paused to take a deep, shuddering breath. 'He had long wavy hair. It looked darker and not so curly as this but smothered in Macassar oil, that would make it straighter and less vivid in colour.'

'Are you sure, dearest? Because if you...'

'I know it was him. And it means he's been here again, lurking around our home. Oh, Albert. Suppose he tries to take me off again, while you're at work?'

He squeezed her hand.

'Then I shan't leave you here alone for the next few days.' Of, course, being suspended meant he could stay at home indefinitely but if Nell thought he was here for her safety's sake, so much the better. He could put off telling her the truth a little longer. Coward, he thought. 'We will investigate this case together; find this red-headed devil,' he told her.

Nell managed a smile.

'Like Mr Holmes and Dr Watson,' she said.

'Who?'

'Dr Conan Doyle's detectives. You remember. You gave me his book, *A Study in Scarlet,* for my birthday.'

'Oh, that. You'll have to tell me about it; I've not read it.'

'We won't have time, too much detecting to do. Besides, what about your work?'

'This will be my work, won't it?'

'The trouble is,' Nell went on, 'Inspector Lestrade of the Yard is a hopeless detective, so I think I will have to be Sherlock Holmes with the magnifying glass...' She peered at him closely through the lens. 'And you'll be my loyal assistant, Dr Watson.'

'Does Dr Watson get to eat twice a day?'

'Of course. Mr Holmes will investigate the local market first thing in the morning and will cook his well-meaning, if rather dull, friend a substantial sausage breakfast before they set about detecting for the day.'

'I'm relieved to hear it.'

As they went upstairs to bed, Albert spoke into the gloom of the narrow stairwell:

'Just how 'dull' is this friend of Mr Holmes?'

'Very.'

Chapter 16

Tuesday, 23rd October

'**D**R WATSON' did indeed get a decent sausage breakfast after Nell had hurried to the local butcher's stall first thing, keeping a sharp lookout on the way for any red-haired villains that might be lurking in the dawn-shadowed alleyways as she passed. Her return was greeted enthusiastically by Blackstock who, smelling meat of some kind, wound himself in a figure of eight around her ankles, flicking the tip of his tail expectantly while mewing like the starving scrap of flea-bitten fur he had once been.

'Later, Blackstock. Albert gets first dibs.'

'And rightly so.' Albert was yawning as he fastened his stiff collar in place on a freshly laundered shirt. The linen smelled of starch with a lingering trace of warmth from Nell's pre-dawn efforts with the smoothing irons. Seeing her in her coat and scarf, he asked: 'Going out? I'll come with you.'

'Too late; I've already been to the market. Look: bacon,

sausages, eggs, a loaf and a can of milk... and mutton chops and carrots for dinner.'

'Nell!' He gripped her arm more roughly than he intended. 'Sorry, but it's not safe for you to go out alone, not with that fiend about.'

'I was careful, kept a wary eye out for him. There was no sign.'

'Don't you dare go out alone again, Nell. I forbid it until he's caught.'

She sighed heavily, glaring at him as she took off her coat and fetched the pan to cook breakfast.

'I won't be a prisoner in my own home just because of him. Besides, being at home didn't s-stop him...' Nell turned away to fill the kettle from the hand-pump over the sink, but Albert could tell by the catch in her voice that she was near to tears.

'It won't be for long, sweetheart,' he said, hugging her from behind, 'He'll soon be behind bars, I promise you.'

With an unladylike sniff, she swallowed down her tears and dabbed at her nose with her cuff. Sometimes, Albert thought, smiling to himself, the flower-girl was still there beneath the demure striped bombazine and spotless linen.

'I love you, Nell,' he whispered into the soft slenderness of her neck. The fine soft curls, like baby hair behind her ear, tickled his nose. 'I just want you to be safe. I'd be lost without you... could never forgive myself if...'

'Stop it, Albert Sutton. Nothing is going to happen to me. I've got you to guard me, haven't I?'

'So long as you remember that and let me protect you and don't go traipsing to the market, alone, at every opportunity. Promise me.'

'I promise. Now let me see about breakfast, else it'll be midday before Holmes and Watson set about tracking down this villain.'

The Grosvenor-Berkeley residence, Primrose Hill

That wretched cat. My face was sore this morning and the scratches difficult to conceal. I had sent Appleby to Harrods first thing to purchase some stage makeup for me. His expression was one of utter dismay that he, a gentleman's gentleman of such repute, should be required to obtain some item so disgustingly common as music-hall face-paint, as he called it. Such stuffs have been charged to my account before when I have required disguises, but they were always ordered by telephone – myself and the Harrods establishment being among the first in the city to acquire such devices of convenience.

But this morning my need was too urgent to await the arrival of a dawdling delivery boy, so Appleby had to go, a veritable picture of righteous chagrin. I might have smiled at the man's discomfiture but an excessively deep cat-scratch across the corner of my mouth, one that was barely scabbed over, made smiling inadvisable, if it was not to commence bleeding anew. Eating and drinking were feats hardly accomplished without considerable inconvenience and discomfort, not to say actual, physical pain.

Westminster

With my injuries shielded from view by assiduously applied layers of makeup, I took a Hansom to Westminster. It was raining, and I wore a wide-brimmed hat, in the style of that ne'er-do-well Oscar Wilde, to preserve the concealing makeup intact from the weather. A deep doorway into an old coaching inn gave me a fair view of Scotland Yard through the squally rain. The battered door behind me was chained and the padlock rusty with disuse. I had waited here on previous occasions and never been disturbed. Opposite, across the mud-slicked cobbles, was the teashop often frequented by my quarry and the tantalising odour of fresh-baked pastries wafted from the curtained window that stood a little ajar.

Sutton was late arriving this morning, unless I had missed him. I felt that was unlikely. If he was too early, Sutton generally went into the tea shop before commencing his day's labour, always entering the police headquarters as Big Ben began to strike the hour of nine. The bell had tolled nine o'clock seventeen minutes since by my fob watch and there was no sign of him.

I was becoming chilled, despite my stylish herringbone shooting coat from Savile Row, with its extra layer of warmth in the shoulder cape and Russian reindeer-skin gloves. I determined that a turn across Hungerford Bridge – an excursion to the unsavoury south-side of the river as a little adventure that would keep my blood circulating and revive the sensations in my feet which had been numbed by the October airs.

As I approached the bridge, deep in thought, the whistle of a train departing Charing Cross Station startled me from my reverie. Belching its head of steam, its wheels sparking upon the rails, it passed close by above me, showering the walkway with coal smuts, besmirching my coat. What fool ever determined that locomotives and pedestrians ought to share a bridge? I should have to write a letter of complaint to the chairman of the South Eastern Railway Company, demanding compensation for the ruination of my attire.

Continuing across the walkway, I became aware of footsteps behind me, keeping pace precisely. There were numerous persons going about their business, despite the inclement weather, but I sensed these dogged footsteps were quite particular, never coming closer nor falling further behind. In the centre of the bridge, I paused, as one might well do to look down and observe the murky waters hastening eastwards beneath. The Thames was on an ebb tide, all manner of flotsam and jetsam carried away: strands of waterweed pulled from its holdfast by the force of the current after the rain; a length of rotting ship's timber and the bloated carcass of a dead animal – dog or cat: it was impossible to identify for certain. I hoped it was a cat: a singular black feline I had in mind.

I glanced back, expecting to observe the miscreant who dared follow me. An elderly fellow limping, leaning on his walking-stick; a street whore hurrying home in her heeled shoes after a night's work; two urchins bowling a rusty wheel-rim like a hoop and shrieking at the tops of their voices and a baker's boy with his covered basket. None had those determined footsteps which shadowed mine.

CHAPTER 17

'**I**T IS definitely him? Are you sure, Nell?' Albert asked as they sipped lukewarm tea in a down-at-heel place opposite Waterloo Station.

'Of course. He looked straight at me and I could just make out the scratches on his face. He's tried to cover them up, but I could see them.' She had set down the heavy-looking basket in which her normal clothes were folded, in case she needed them. A loaf of bread peeped out from beneath the covering cloth. Having removed her flat cap, her hair was coming loose from its net and she tucked the errant strands behind her ear. She fidgeted on her chair, not used to wearing a man's worsted trousers. They were Albert's old gardening trousers – not that he ever so much as pulled up a dandelion, though he did cut their little square of grass with a sickle, occasionally. The trousers had to be rolled up at the bottom and tied with string around her waist. The moth-eaten muffler and short jacket were his too. Only the apron was her own. 'This tea tastes like... I don't know what: river water.'

'I agree. Not a patch on Mrs Mumbles', is it?' Albert sat hunched and bent over his teacup, his hair whitened with flour – he reminded Nell of her grandfather.

Having seen their 'subject of interest', as Albert referred to the man, turn and retrace his steps over the bridge, presumably to return to his doorway to continue keeping watch, they had thought it too suspicious if they followed him back again. Instead, they had taken refuge from the rain, which was falling harder now, to have a well-deserved cuppa and a brief sit down in this shoddy little place which smelled of mouldy potatoes and last week's herrings. At least it was dry although the meagre fire in the grate spat and hissed on wet coal, giving out more smoke than warmth.

'I cannot believe he had the audacity to be hanging about outside the Yard. Is he spying on me, do you think?'

'Most certainly.'

'I cannot imagine why.'

'I told you, Albert, he was watching out for you, so it's fortunate you're not working there today, else he would be following you, instead of us following him. 'Surveillance' do you call it?'

'Surveillance, yes. He obviously hasn't heard that I've been suspended from duty,' Albert said, draining the last of the weak, tepid tea. He set his empty cup down slowly, the soft chink of china on china echoing in the deathly silence of realisation. 'I'm sorry – '

'Suspended – ' They both spoke at once.

'I meant to tell you.'

'But you didn't! Albert, how could you not tell me? What happened? Why did they suspend you? What are we going to do? How will you get your job back? This is terrible.' Nell pushed her chair back, scraping the uneven flagged floor and rucking up a threadbare rug in shades of puce and grey. 'Why didn't you tell me?' she cried.

Then she was gone, her disguise forgotten, her basket still on the floor beside the tea-table. A customer coughed and cleared his throat loudly to cover his embarrassment.

Albert watched Nell through the grimy, rain-streaked window, fleeing back across the bridge, her hair streaming free of its net. He straightened himself to his full height, relieving the ache in his back from stooping over for hours, but nothing could relieve the pain in his heart on seeing her run from him. Like a timid woodland creature whose trust he had earned by years of patience, now all was undone in a few words; trust destroyed.

He threw his last sixpence on the table to pay for the tea, not bothering to retrieve it when it rolled off and bounced onto the floor. Abandoning the walking-stick, he went out into the cold autumn rain.

CHAPTER 18

**Wednesday, 24ᵗʰ October
Summerlea Villas**

NELL WAS pegging out the sheets on the washing line, strung across their little garden. This morning, an insipid-looking sun was attempting to force its way through the thin, grey veil of cloud. Nell hoped it would be sufficient to dry the sheets. Blackstock was tip-toeing around the edge of the grassy square, doing his best not to get his fur wet from the yellowing tufts that were still soaked from yesterday's rain.

Usually, Nell enjoyed her work and would be singing to herself as she went about her chores. But not this morning.

Albert was in the kitchen, engrossed in *The Times*, annoyed to read that there had been a jewel theft on his patch the night before, with a couple left for dead in their parlour as a result. The newspaper reporter had learned of it and written about the crime in salacious detail, yet he, Inspector Albert Sutton, remained completely ignorant of the case, on suspension. That a mere reporter had the facts and he did not, quite put him off his breakfast – much to the glee of Blackstock who'd finished off the kipper, although he'd turned his nose up at the remains of Nell's fish, not appreciating the strawberry jam she'd smeared on it.

The incident of the theft alone, though, didn't fully account for Albert's ill-humour nor for Nell's abandonment of her singing: the couple had barely exchanged more than the odd monosyllable since yesterday, at that gloomy teashop. The conversation upon their return home had gone something like this:

'Sorry,' said Albert, dumping the covered washing basket with its single loaf of bread that he had carried home like a delivery boy.

'Tea?' asked Nell, who had been relieved to get out of her wet men's clothing into a dry skirt.

'Please.'

'How long?'

'My suspension?'

Nell nodded as she poured the tea. Albert shrugged.

'Don't know.'

'Why?'

'Does it matter?'

'No.'

That had been the gist of their exchanges ever since and they hardly made for a happy home.

Blackstock wound his way between Nell's ankles, desperate for her attention. When he didn't get it, he jumped into the washing basket, his muddy paws kneading the spotless cotton sheets.

'Oh, Blackstock! How could you?' Nell sighed at the thought of having to wash them again. 'You naughty cat.' He stared at her with his great luminous green eyes, a picture of innocence, even as he sat at the scene of his crime. She picked him up, hugging him close, murmuring 'bad cat' into his coal-dark fur as the tears came. 'What am I going to do, Blackstock? Albert doesn't trust me. He won't even tell me why he was suspended. I'm sure he never did anything wrong. We'll be penniless soon with him not working. I'll have to take in washing: more laundry for you to muddy, you bad, bad cat. What am I going to do?'

~

Despite yesterday's very damp and relatively purposeless observations outside Scotland Yard, matters have since come to light that I find most gratifying. It came to pass that I overheard certain officers of the law as they departed the Yard, without any sense of discretion whatever, discussing in loud tones the suspension of their colleague, Inspector Sutton, *without pay*. Thus, his absence was explained and the subtle progress of my plans for him revealed, precisely as intended. If suspension and poverty do not drive him to the brink, then I shall have misjudged my victim – an extraordinarily unlikely eventuality.

Since observation at the Yard will no longer serve any purpose, it is needful, henceforth, to maintain a watch upon his house. To that end, I shall require a new disguise. It would be a grievous loss were he to take his life and I was not there to witness the event. Surely, his demise cannot now be long delayed?

In the meantime, to avoid tedium, I have in mind a brief experiment with an alternative specimen – one that has required elimination for a while: that detestably silent former butler at St John's. Since his dismissal at my insistence, I had made enquiries as to the wretch's whereabouts. Other club members, unaccountably, even knew his name: Maurice Culpepper. Quite undeservedly, the fellow had already been employed in the same capacity as a butler at Brown's of St James. Clearly, I should have written a letter to them, informing them of his dire unsuitability and their grave error. But then it occurred to me that I might spare the waste of ink and paper, the time taken and the cost of a stamp by removing the offending lackey.

With this tantalising thought lightening my mood, I took my pistol from the drawer in my study and ordered my brougham to be brought to the door. So ebullient were my spirits and knowing how Fortune so often favoured my activities, I wondered if my path might cross that of a particularly loathsome feline, now that I had my pistol in my pocket. Not that I would seek it out – it wasn't worth the effort – but if the opportunity presented itself, who could say what might occur? But that was for later. First, in order to witness another of my 'incidents' of calamity for ex-Inspector Sutton, I had to don another elaborate disguise.

~

'Albert. Are you listening to me?'

'What is it, Nell?' Albert was reading his newspaper for the second time that morning, still trying to find something interesting but innocuous enough that it did not bring his seething anger back to boiling point.

'I've remembered something, about the day I was kidnapped.'

'Oh?' This was indeed of interest. Or might be. He folded his paper and put it aside.

'The zoo. I could hear the animals.'

'When?'

'As I ran from that hateful place. I'd climbed the wall...'

'You did what, Nell?'

'What choice did I have? It was my only means of escape. No time to play the grand lady and I don't care if you disapprove.'

'No, I suppose you're right. Go on.'

'Well, I ran down a hill. I could see London in the

distance, but it wasn't too far. I knew I had to get home. It was all grass and trees and sky. Then I crossed a road with big houses, into another grassy place. And I came to the canal. It was there I heard the animals. I'm sure it's the zoo you took me to back in the summer, where we ate our sandwiches while watching the tiger and we had a ride on that smelly camel. You remember?'

'Of course. How could I forget? We bought ice-creams from an Italian fellow on a bicycle with an ice box on the back. Very good they were too.' Albert went to a drawer in the dresser and began rummaging beneath beautifully ironed tablecloths and tea-towels. 'It's here somewhere, I know.'

'What are you looking for?'

'A map of London. It must be here.'

Nell went straight to the pantry, moved the breadbin, took out a cloth-bound map of the city and gave it to him.

'What's it doing in there?' Albert asked, unfolding the unwieldy thing and spreading it across the kitchen table.

Nell shrugged.

'That's where you put it. Shall I make us a pot of tea? We can still afford that, can't we?'

Albert didn't answer, busy tracing routes across the map with his finger before turning the whole thing over.

'Ah. Here we are: Victoria Station.'

'Yes. I passed that too,' Nell said, measuring out tea from the caddy into the pot, being sparing with the precious dried leaves.

'Of course you did. It's only round the corner. Now. Come here. Look at the map. See if we can retrace your route.'

Nell frowned at the map. The dots and squares and coloured lines seemed to dance before her eyes.

'We're here,' Albert pointed, 'At Carlisle Place. This is Buckingham Palace and here's Mayfair.' He tapped the map. 'And Curzon Square where you used to work. Now show me from which direction you came.'

Nell stared blankly at the vast sheet – big enough for a counterpane for the bed but how could all of London fit on it? How could Buckingham Palace be here, in her kitchen?

'I don't know, Albert. I don't understand.' She looked at him, her eyes brimming with tears. 'I'm sorry. I just don't know.' Sobbing, she gathered up her skirts, fled the kitchen and bolted up the stairs.

Women! Who could make head or tail of their feelings? He certainly couldn't. Nell hadn't always been this prone to tears. What was wrong with her these days?

The kettle came to the boil, but Albert ignored its hissing, slumped at the table. What an idiot he was. Poor Nell had never looked at a map before. Why should she? No wonder she was confused. In disgust, he began to refold the map only to have the stubborn thing refuse to accept his efforts to use the original creases. Stupid damned map! In a temper, he bundled it into a heap and shoved it back in the pantry, closing the door swiftly to prevent its escape. What good was a map to someone who didn't understand it?

To calm himself and soothe his temper, he finally made the tea.

～

Eventually, Nell came back downstairs, red-eyed. Without a word, Albert poured her some tea: a peace offering.

'I've been looking out the bedroom window,' Nell said, 'There's an old woman outside in the street. I have seen her three or four times, going up and down.'

'Is she committing a crime?' Albert was wary of getting involved, seeing his circumstances at present, preferring the safer occupation of reading his newspaper – yet again.

'No, but I think it seems sus – '

'Then she is of no account to us, Nell. Best leave well alone.'

'She looks... I don't know... furtive, somehow.'

'Why don't you find something useful to do, besides questioning everybody else's business?' Albert said, flinging aside the newspaper, so pages were spread across the floor, all out of order.

The sudden banging at the front door made them both jump. Nell looked at Albert with a puzzled frown.

'If it's Maudie Cooper, we can sort this out once and for...'

'It won't be, whoever she is,' Albert said, straightening his waistcoat as he went along the hall. 'And if it's that woman you saw from the window, she can damn well clear off too. We don't have money to spare for charity, any longer.'

No sooner had he opened the door than a large hobnail boot was planted on the threshold to prevent any chance of closure.

'Mr Albert Sutton?' A heavy set fellow with the misshapen nose and cauliflower ears of a bare-knuckle boxer touched his forelock. Yet it was hardly a gesture of subservience, more an act of defiance. Another equally intimidating man stood on the steps behind him.

'Yes. I'm Albert Sutton. Who are you? What business do you have, coming to my door all unexpectedly?'

'The name's 'Obbs, George 'Obbs: court-appointed bailiff. So's 'Arry Martin.' He gestured over his shoulder. 'We've come t' collect yer rent wots late bein' paid.'

'But the rent isn't late. It's not due until the first of the month. Now get off my doorstep.' Albert tried to close the door, but Hobbs now had both feet firmly over the doorsill, standing on the 'welcome' mat in the hall. Martin was close behind and Albert saw with dismay the knuckle-duster on the second man's fist as he polished it on his lapel.

'Landlord don't agree. Nor does the beak.'

'The case has gone before a magistrate already? That's ridiculous. The courts just don't work that fast. Besides, there is no case to answer.'

'We're to collect four pounds, eighteen shillings and four pence. It's last month's overdues and next month's in advance. Payment in full, landlord wants, or yer owt!'

'*You* can get out; both of you. You made a mistake; got the wrong address.'

'We never make mistakes, do we 'Arry? It's defaulters like you wot make the mistake. Court says you owe, so we come t' collect.'

'But the rent is only seventeen shillings and sixpence.'

'Landlord says it's gawn up, plus court fees, plus interest fer ev'ry day it's late.'

'This is monstrous!' Albert cried, verging on despair.

Across the street, an elderly lady was watching, laughing behind the veil of her widow's bonnet.

Nell dashed to the door, bringing the rent book. Albert showed the bailiff the last page: all neatly recorded and up to date, the most recent payment made on 1st October.

'That's as may be,' Hobbs said with a shrug. 'Anyone can write a few numbers in a book. You got t' 'ave proof you paid in full.'

'This is proof. We have paid in full.' Albert shook the little book in Hobbs's face, but the man snatched it from him and tossed it into the street. 'How dare you...'

'Landlord wants it paid in advance now. Word's got round you lost yer job and he don't rent t' no ex-coppers wiv no job. Does 'e, 'Arry?' The other man cracked his fingers and grinned. 'We'll wait one more day. This time t'morrow, you pay up or me an' 'Arry an' a few mates'll chuck you and yer pretty piece out on yer arses. Understand? Till t'morrow, then. Come on, 'Arry. Let's go get paid: we done our bit.'

The elderly lady was elated to see Sutton come down

the steps to retrieve his rent book, his face a picture of abject misery. Matters were proceeding so well.

'Have they gone?' Nell asked, a tremor in her voice. Albert slammed the door, scowling fit to turn butter rancid. 'The brutes scared me so, Albert. Will they be back?'

He didn't answer. He knew he should comfort his frightened wife, reassure her, but he was too angry.

'Shall I make us some tea?' She sounded so timid. Tea? Damn it. He needed something stronger than that.

'I'm going out.'

'But where are you going?'

'What does it matter to you, woman? Keep your interfering nose out of it, can't you? You've got no idea how much I...' His voice tailed off. His temper had exploded again.

With his coat over his arm and his battered old gardening cap in his hand, he stormed down the hall and was gone, slamming the front door so hard that the house shook.

Covering the ground at such a ferocious pace, by the time he was two streets away, Albert had an acute stitch in his side and was forced to slow down. But it didn't ease the pain and, besides, he hadn't bothered to button his coat and now he was both cold and sweating. Foolish: he would catch a chill if he wasn't careful but, to be honest, he wasn't sure if he cared.

The Coach and Horses, the public house on the corner, looked warm and inviting, a haven of cheerfulness. Albert searched his pockets and found a penny three farthings – enough for a drink or two of the cheapest sort, at least.

The tankard of beer was weak as rainwater so, with the last of his coins, he bought a tot of gin instead. It scoured his throat and scorched his gullet as it went down and did nothing whatever to lighten his mood. Worry about paying the bailiffs, loss of his job, regret at the things he'd said to

Nell: all weighed him down. Words had poured from his lips like pus from an abscess, poisoning their love for each other as surely as a dose of arsenic. She hadn't deserved that, but the words could never be unsaid. Why couldn't he keep his temper? Why did he vent his misery on her? She was not to blame for his situation yet he was making her suffer too. Head in hands, he lingered long over the last few drops of gin.

The elderly woman in a widow's bonnet had come in a while after Albert. Respectable ladies never frequented such places, not even when escorted by gentlemen, but she seemed at ease, sitting in the shadowed corner of the public bar, nursing her gin as the ancient timepiece on the wall ticked away the hours until closing time. Her alert expression and piercing gaze behind her veil belied her age as she watched Albert. He was quite unaware of her keen observation of him, her over-large hands dappled with the freckles of a red-head and a self-satisfied smile lurking at the corner of her thin-lipped mouth.

~

Nell had followed Albert at a distance, having to trot along to keep up and not lose sight of him. The feeble October sun glistened on the cobbles in the side streets and turned the muddy puddles to sepia mirrors in the gutter. She was worried about Albert; had never seen him in such a temper. He would probably scold her again for her 'interfering nose', but she had to make certain he didn't do anything foolish.

A chilly breeze tugged at her hat as she waited outside the *Coach and Horses*, watching customers come and go, stamping her feet and blowing on her hands – she should have worn her gloves. An elderly woman paused at the door of the public house, glancing around before going inside. It was the momentary hesitation that caught Nell's eye:

wasn't that the same woman she'd seen wandering up and down outside their house that morning? 'Furtive': that was how she'd described the woman to Albert and now she was even more convinced. The woman was ragged as a beggar and bent with age, yet her clothes were well filled out by a body far from gaunt, the cheeks plump enough and, had she stood straight, so Nell estimated, she would have been near as tall as Albert. A disguise: that was it. It couldn't be that horrible man again, dressed as a woman, could it? Or was one of Albert's police colleagues following him? The more she thought about it, the more certain Nell became.

Then something brushed against her skirts and Nell looked down.

'Blackstock, you followed me.' She bent to stroke his fur. He purred in appreciation, rumbling like a wooden-wheeled barrow on a rutted road. 'I suppose you think it's dinnertime, don't you? Well, you'll have to wait. Go and catch yourself a mouse, if you're so hungry: that's what cats are supposed to do. You're getting fat and lazy, you are.'

The cat continued to weave himself around her ankles. He felt warm against her cold ankles and Nell appreciated that so made no effort to shoo him away. The resulting cat hairs on woollen stockings would be a small price to pay.

Albert came out of the public house and hurried around the corner. Nell moved so she could see him going down the side street before disappearing into the alleyway behind the building. She could guess why – a glass of beer always went straight to his bladder. Blackstock recognised the possibility of another friendly food source and darted across the road to follow Albert just as the old woman came out of the door with the same intention. The two came face to face: the cat and the woman. Blackstock froze, his fur on end, his tail pointing to the sky. Bristling, he looked three times his usual size. The woman moved to step by him. Blackstock hissed. She tried to move into the gutter.

Blackstock arched his back and spat at her. Nell watched, fascinated. The cat obviously had the same concerns about the woman as she did.

The woman began rummaging in her reticule, but Blackstock flew at her, hissing and clawing. She cried out. Albert came running, just in time to see the woman lose her balance with the force of the cat's impact against her chest and fall to the pavement. It was like the madhouse at Bedlam. The woman was cursing and flailing; Albert was shouting and trying to get hold of the squirming animal, grabbing fistfuls of fur, but Blackstock clung on, still spitting and hissing. Albert got bitten and let go, staggered back a step and stumbled over the woman's large well-shod feet. The woman tried to get up, but Blackstock renewed his attack, clawing at her face.

A crowd was gathering. A distant police whistle blew. Nell waded in to help Albert, softly calling to Blackstock in the hope of calming him. Two policemen – one of them was Constable Michaelson – were now on the scene to assist. Albert stopped sucking at his bitten thumb, took off his coat and threw it over the cat. With its ferocious yowls now muffled by the thick Harris tweed, he succeeded in pulling the cat off the woman. But the animal had not released its hold and her bonnet and a bundle of grey hair came away. She wore a wig. Albert was about to start apologising profusely until he saw the woman's face. She was scratched and bitten, but not all the injuries were new: some were plastered over with thick makeup.

'Mr Cornhill?' Albert said, recognising, despite its condition, the face of the man who had reported his wife missing, days ago. 'James Cornhill of Inkerman Terrace? Whatever are you doing dressed so?'

Constable Michaelson helped the man up off the pavement. The crowd was intrigued and pressed forward.

Nell squeezed through to Albert's side, holding

Blackstock wrapped tightly in her husband's coat. Seeing Cornhill, she gasped.

'That's him! That's the man who had me kidnapped! Arrest him, Albert!'

'Are you sure, Nell?'

'Yes. Just look at his hair: long, reddish and curly; like the one we found tangled in Blackstock's claws.'

'She is being utterly absurd; melodramatic; ridiculous,' Cornhill said, brushing himself down. It was no easy matter to sound in command of the situation, dressed as a beggar-woman. 'She's having an attack of the vapours, the foolish woman. She does not know me from Adam. I am the one who should be complaining: that wretched beast ought to be destroyed immediately. This woman is simply attempting to divert attention from the creature.'

'But he's got red hair and his face has been scratched before,' Nell insisted, tears threatening. 'Blackstock wouldn't attack unless he was provoked. And why is he in disguise? He was following my husband.'

'Preposterous talk. Utter nonsense, every word,' Cornhill said.

A well-dressed man stepped forward from the crowd.

'But I know you: I've seen you at St John's Club in Mayfair.'

'An' I've seen 'im at the music 'all, at the *Lyceum*, ain't I, sir?' said a woman with wild-looking hair and impossibly crimson lips. The policemen inched closer to Mr Cornhill, one on each side of him.

'Are you absolutely certain, Nell?' Albert asked, 'Because if you are...'

Nell nodded.

'I'm not likely to forget the man who had me bundled in a box and taken to his house and manhandled me. It's him. No doubt about it.'

'Officers: arrest this man; take him in charge,' Albert said.

'Yes, Mr Sutton, sir.' The policemen grabbed him and there was a struggle. A pistol appeared from the folds of Cornhill's shabby skirt and a shot fired, gashing the sleeve of Constable Michaelson's uniform. The crowd drew back a little, but they need not have worried. It was soon all over as Albert and the policemen overpowered the prisoner and the pistol skittered into the gutter.

Since everyone else was concerned with the scuffle, Nell retrieved the weapon and tucked it in her pocket.

'I know who you are,' said the well-dressed man. 'I remember now: you are Grosvenor-Berkeley! Upon my word, sir, what a rum lark is this? You're a molly, dressed like a street-walker... whatever next?' The man began to laugh. The prisoner smiled.

'Of course, I am Lord Grosvenor-Berkeley, at your service,' he said, bowing to the crowd: his audience. 'This is all a most ridiculous mistake. Chief Constable Williamson and Assistant Commissioner Anderson are fellow club members and I shall see to it that they hear of this-this débâcle before the day is done. As for you, Sutton, you cannot arrest me since you are suspended from duty, pending investigation.'

Albert was too shocked to speak. How did this fellow know that?

It was Constable Michaelson who answered:

'That is irrelevant, sir. I am arresting you for assaulting a constable with a deadly weapon, namely a pistol, while in pursuance of his duty. That constable being myself. And I have all these witnesses...' The policeman indicated the crowd which was nodding and agreeing.

Without warning, the man wrenched free of Michaelson's grasp, clutched up his skirts and bolted. Whistles blowing, the constables were off in pursuit with

Albert, Nell and everyone else close behind. Not to be left out, Blackstock leapt up onto a high wall to take a shortcut to the front of the chase as it headed towards Victoria Station.

CHAPTER 19

ALBERT WAS dismayed to see Cornhill, Grosvenor-Berkeley or whatever his name was, disappear into the maw of Victoria Railway Station. Sunlight struggled through the soot-caked glass roof, leaving the station in a perpetual gloom that the gas lamps – far from illuminating – seemed to make darker, somehow, the six long platforms, the ten sets of silver rails snaking out, into the distance beyond the massive covering roof. An engine hooted, a whistle blew as a train in the London, Brighton & South Coast Railway livery of ochre and olive-green belched steam and began to move, destined for Robertsbridge, Hastings and St Leonards, so the chalkboard informed Albert. He hoped the man they were pursuing hadn't managed to board that train. No, not enough time to have bought a ticket, always supposing he was honest enough to do so.

The concourse was bustling and there were queues at the ticket offices: city gentlemen in bowler hats, armed with black rolled umbrellas, just in case; couples going to Brighton on honeymoon who kept giving each other coy, uncertain smiles; frail elderly folk in bath-chairs with their nursemaids, off to Tunbridge Wells or Worthing for convalescence. But there was no sign of the fellow in his tattered skirts, queuing with the rest. Constables Michaelson and Parker, in their official capacity, were making enquiries of the porters and station staff but Albert watched and saw shaken heads all around. There was a moment of hope as a porter pointed to someone at the special ticket office for those wishing to travel in the greater comfort of the Pullman trains, but a glance was sufficient to dispel that hope. The woman in question was indeed elderly and somewhat dishevelled in appearance, but such a tiny, birdlike creature was most certainly not the one they sought.

Nell and many of the pursuing crowd arrived in ones and twos, some breathless, on the verge of collapse, others red-faced and perspiring, depending on their general state of health and their eagerness to be in at the kill, so to speak. The gaudy woman from the *Lyceum* was fanning her face with her gloves, her face make-up blotched with sweat.

'Cor, that was a run,' she puffed, 'Where's he gawn then? Did I miss him, the ol' bugger?'

'That Grosvenor-Berkeley fellow'll bring the club into disrepute, behaving like a scoundrel,' said the St John's club member, mopping his brow with a blue kerchief. 'Upon my soul, what a to-do this is. Have they caught him yet?'

Albert shook his head.

'I'm afraid not, sir. The miscreant is still at large, but we'll get him.'

'Well, I cannot waste time any longer. I need a stiff brandy after all this.'

'You may be called as a witness, sir, to the events. I'll need your name and address, sir, if you would oblige me...' Albert's words were drowned out by the arrival of the 1.47 from Brighton, but in the time it took him to get out his notebook and pencil, the man had vanished into the crowd disembarking from the train. 'Grosvenor-Berkeley...?'

Something had caught Albert's attention, if he could only remember what, precisely. Things had happened so fast, he needed to take a few minutes to calm and compose himself; to think.

He grasped Nell's arm and led her across the concourse, weaving their way through the swirling crowd of people, arriving, departing or just waiting, to the *Station Buffet*. The place looked grand enough, the name painted above the door in gold letters a foot high, lots of highly-polished mahogany and gleaming brasswork, but the reputation of railway catering was poor indeed. The renowned Savoy chef, Alexis Soyez, had once described station coffee as being 'about as bad as a human being could possibly make it'. So Albert ordered tea, in the hope the buffet would do a better job of that, without a second thought as to how he might pay for it.

As they were sipping their hot tea – which wasn't too bad at all – Albert kept one eye on the people passing by or milling about on the other side of the window glass. He recognised a near-neighbour from Carlisle Place, carrying a suitcase, and a lad he'd once arrested for pick-pocketing. He watched the lad following his neighbour – probably up to his old tricks, again. The neighbour was hastening towards the Victoria Street exit. Albert saw the sign, but then he forgot all about his neighbour being a possible target of crime as he read a second sign which pointed the way to the *Grosvenor Hotel*. The luxurious hotel had been built above the station. Surely, it was not a coincidence that the great establishment shared its name with the man who had kidnapped Nell? Did the wretch own the place? Was that possible?

The *Grosvenor Hotel*

I was hardly suitably attired for the Imperial Suite. I had worn a good shirt and morning trousers beneath the rags, but without a jacket and tie, the manager would have turned me out, and rightly so, had he not recognised me, even in my distress. In which case, of course, the Imperial Suite was immediately at my disposal. My mother's family did have its uses occasionally, my Great-Uncle Ezekiel Grosvenor's ownership of the hotel being one of them. I had discarded my ragged clothing behind the kitchens, before using the tradesmen's entrance – a humiliating necessity in the circumstances.

Now I was safe: the staff would deny having seen me, if they valued their positions, not to mention their lives, and my name did not appear in the register. I would bathe, telephone Appleby to send around clean attire, dine and have a good night's rest in the palatial suite. Tomorrow, or maybe the day following, I would take the Pullman train to Brighton, visit the Prince of Wales at the Pavilion, perhaps. Only last month we had been at a shooting party together and he had invited me to join him at any time. I would take the sea air for a few days and return when the trail had gone cold and the Metropolitan Police grown weary of the chase – their interest would wane swiftly, I was certain.

∼

Nell found the clothes in the alleyway behind the hotel kitchens, in amongst vegetable peelings and fish guts.

'It was Blackstock who discovered them,' Nell told Albert and Constable Michaelson, 'I thought he was after a few fish heads for supper but no; he found the dress. Who needs a bloodhound when we've got Blackstock?' She held the cat in her arms. He purred loudly as she praised him and nuzzled the soft black fur below his ear. 'You're a clever cat, aren't you? An extra helping for you tonight.'

'But where did the devil go? Now we don't even know what he's wearing.' Albert was inwardly fuming: if only he'd thought of the hotel sooner.

'Well, if he's stark naked we'd have no trouble... beggin' yer pardon, Mrs Sutton,' the constable joked.

'Go in there, Michaelson, demand to see the hotel register.'

'Me, sir? But I'm only an 'umble constable...'

'And I'm an inspector on suspension with no legal authorisation, Michaelson, so hop to it, or do we have to await Parker's return with reinforcements and another inspector, eh?'

'No, sir, I'll ask.'

'You will 'demand', constable, if you ever hope to become a sergeant.'

Straightening his uniform and sighing in dismay over the gash in the sleeve where the bullet had rent the cloth, Michaelson marched towards the grand marbled atrium. The doorman did not doff his high hat, nor did he open the mighty portal for the policeman, but at least he made no attempt to bar his way.

Albert and Nell waited on the steps by a huge potted palm in a terracotta urn the size of a Hansom cab. The pale daylight was fast-fading into a chill, dreary dusk. Albert realised they had rushed from the *Station Buffet* without settling the bill so now he truly had committed a crime. He would have to return and make amends but knew his pockets were empty, yet he dare not allow the slightest stain on his already-sullied reputation. It really was too bad how his situation became worse at every turn.

Nell was hungry, having had nothing but that cup of railway-buffet tea since breakfast but she knew better than to mention it to her husband. It was obvious from the severity of his scowl, his lips pursed thinner than a shoelace and his fists thrust into the depths of his pockets that Albert was in a foul temper – again. And it became fouler still when Constable Michaelson reported that there were no suspicious-looking names, aliases or pseudonyms to be seen in the register of the *Grosvenor Hotel*.

Suspension be damned. Albert stormed into the atrium, brushing aside the efforts of the lugubrious doorman to actually do his duty, and rapped on the high counter in reception. Taking his own good time, the lackey behind the counter turned.

'Good evening, sir, madam, how may I be of assistance to you?' The voice oozed like treacle.

'I will see the register... now,' Albert said.

'Ah, would that be the register I but lately showed to the constable, sir? I will require to see your authority to make such a demand. The register is not a public document.'

'I am an inspector with the Metropolitan Police...'

'Then you will have a warrant card, I believe they call it. May I see yours, sir?' The man was right to ask, of course, but Albert's warrant card was locked in Chief Constable Williamson's bottom drawer, gathering dust alongside his other official belongings: his old notebooks and whistle. Even his truncheon; not that he used the latter items very often, now he was no longer a Bobby on the beat, but they were precious to him all the same. He wondered if he would ever have them returned to him.

'Very well.' Albert cleared his throat noisily. 'In that case, my wife and I wish to book a room for the night.'

Nell gasped, knowing Albert had used their last tuppence halfpenny, scraped together from purse-corners and pocket-depths, to pay for their tea in the café at Waterloo on Tuesday. She wasn't sure how Albert had managed to buy any drink at the *Coach and Horses* earlier, unless he'd found a coin in the road, missed by the street-sweepers. And she couldn't recall now that he'd paid their bill at the *Station Buffet* either. How on earth could they afford a night in this grand hotel? The cost must be extortionate.

'I see,' said the man behind the counter, 'And sir will be paying in advance?'

'No. Put it on an account made out to the Metropolitan Police.'

'Very well, sir. You will be required to sign the register.'

'I know.' Albert was triumphant as he took the heavy ledger in its gold-embossed cover of crimson leather. Behind the counter, an ornate glass-fronted cabinet held all the room keys. Albert had already counted nineteen keys missing from the hooks beneath the room numbers. He scanned the register, dipped the pen in the gilt inkwell on the counter but took his time about signing. Alongside each signature in the book was noted the number of the room allocated to the guest. On the whole, it was done logically, the rooms on the ground floor, 4-9, were occupied, as were those on the first floor, 10-19: that accounted for sixteen room keys. Room 21: the Presidential Suite, was presently occupied by Sir Irwin Bland 'impresario', whoever he was; and room 24: the Queen's Suite, was booked by the Duke of Sutherland. With a flourish, he added 'Mr & Mrs L.A.D. Sutton' who had been allocated room 2 – probably the broom cupboard, Albert thought – to the bottom of the list. Yet the key to room 30, the Imperial Suite on the top floor, was also missing from the cabinet. Albert had a feeling about that, a prickling of the hairs at the back of his neck.

'Sir has luggage?'

'No luggage.'

'Excuse me, sir, but that's most irregular.'

'First time for everything.'

'And sir, er, there are no animals permitted in this hotel without prior arrangement with the management.' The man indicated Blackstock who sat neatly by Nell's feet, tail curled, looking like an obsidian statue, on his best behaviour for once.

'Then make the arrangement with the management now,' Albert said, urging Nell towards the gilded ironwork cage that was the hotel lift, guarded by a footman in red livery.

'Sir, you'll find room 2 is on the ground floor.' But Albert was already ordering the footman to take the lift to the top.

CHAPTER 20

IT HAD seemed like a brilliant idea at that moment but, as the lift wheezed, creaked and rattled its way up to the third floor of the *Grosvenor Hotel*, there was time enough for doubts to invade Albert's thoughts. What on earth was a detective on suspension, his wife and a tomcat going to do exactly? For certain, he should have taken Nell and the moggy to the safety of their room first. This was no business for a woman, yet one glance at Nell, standing beside him, full of excitement at her first journey in the lift, cat in arms, told him she was not to be left behind now. Her eyes sparkled with anticipation, her face aglow, her demeanour full of eagerness for the chase, like a rider when the hunting-horn sounds the tally-ho.

'Here, Albert: you take Blackstock,' Nell said, interrupting his thoughts. 'I think it would be best if I go to the door first.' She thrust the cat at him. He fumbled with the writhing mass of unco-operative fur.

'You'll do no such thing, Nell, it isn't right.'

'But I'm the one playing Sherlock Holmes, here. Remember, you're only my assistant, Doctor Watson.'

The footman sniggered behind an immaculately-gloved hand; a reminder that they were not alone. Albert felt his face flush. Only Doctor Watson, eh?

'I forbid it, Nell. This is no parlour game,' he said as the lift clunked to a halt and the footman wrestled open the gilded iron gate.

Nell turned to face him in the corridor as the lift began its descent.

'What's *your* plan, then?' she asked.

Albert was still trying to keep a grip on Blackstock and couldn't think properly. Then the cat squirmed and leapt out of his arms. It bolted for the stairs and disappeared on silent paws, down the dimly-lit stairwell. Nell made to follow.

'He'll do well enough,' Albert told her, relieved to be rid of the animal.

'Yes, I know he will, but I need to find the linen cupboard; it's part of my plan.'

'You have one?'

'Of course but we should have found out where they keep the clean sheets and towels, first.'

'It's too dangerous for you, Nell, I can't allow...'

'You haven't even heard my plan yet.'

As they made their way back downstairs, Nell revealed her scheme for getting into the Imperial Suite, to discover who was its unnamed occupant. Albert was forced to admit, at least to himself, that it was better than any idea of his – especially since he didn't have one – but that didn't mean he approved of his wife's insane little ruse. Still, disguise had worked rather well for Grosvenor-Berkeley himself, at least until Blackstock had intervened: it might work in this case too, but he didn't like the risk to Nell if it was Grosvenor-Berkeley on the other side of that door.

Albert wasn't surprised when they discovered the linen cupboard, clearly labelled, right next to their own humble room 2. Servants' quarters, he thought. The door was not locked and inside the space was as neat and orderly as the linen store in a great house. Snowy white bed sheets were piled high on the shelves to the left, each set accompanied by pillow-slips, embroidered in the corner with the Grosvenor monogram. Tablecloths, napkins and towels, similarly adorned, were stacked on the right. But Nell went straight to the wooden racks directly facing the door. Hanging there was a selection of uniforms for the staff, from doormen and page boys, to wine waiters, chefs and chambermaids. Nell took off her coat, folded it neatly and set it down on the floor, putting her hat on top. Then she went along the rack until she found a dress of dark green cloth in a suitable size.

'I hope this is a chamber maid's uniform, or else I could be making an awful mistake. Turn your back, Albert.'

'But I'm your husband.'

'Don't argue. I shall want your unbiased opinion in a minute.'

With a sigh, Albert did as he was told. Skirts rustled; cloth whispered.

'How do I look?' Albert turned to see Nell, demure in the servant's uniform, her lustrous hair hidden under a neat lace-edged cap and a starched pinafore disguised her trim waistline. She wore a stern expression befitting a disgruntled house-keeper. He hardly recognised his pretty wife.

'Well...' he said, tucking one last wayward strand of auburn hair out of sight, beneath the cap, 'Truth is, Nell, I think you'll do, but I still don't like the idea.'

'But you'll be right behind me, won't you, husband, dear, so I shan't be in any danger whatsoever, shall I?'

'Of course, I'll be there, but...'

'No 'buts', Albert.' She gave him a quick kiss on the cheek. 'Now come along, help me with these towels. I shall need a large pile of them. Oh, and you might be wanting this.'

To Albert's astonishment, his wife thrust a small pistol into his hand.

'Good Lord, Nell. What are you doing with this? Where did you get it?'

'It's his: the one he fired at Constable Michaelson. I picked it up when he dropped it during the struggle. I thought you might have need of it.'

Albert put it in his inside pocket, having no intention of using it.

~

I was not pleased to be disturbed from my thoughts by a knock at the door of the Imperial Suite. My intentions for removing that one-time butler at St John's had already been thwarted by the loss of my pistol when those fools attempted to apprehend me. The pistol was a fine little piece, handcrafted in Germany, and I was saddened at the possibility that those uncouth barbarians at the Met must now have it in their grubby hands. It had become necessary to implement some other means of dispatch for the butler – Culpepper, or whatever his absurd name was. Then, to the augmentation of my annoyance, the knock was repeated twice more.

'Who is it? Why are you disturbing me in this manner?'

'Begging your pardon, sir,' a woman's voice called out. 'But it's house-keeping... got it wrong again, sir. Sorry to bother you, sir.'

'I do not require any 'house-keeping'. Now go away.'

'I've brought your clean towels, sir.'

'I have not yet used the towels. Now go away, you foolish woman.'

'But they're yesterday's towels, sir. Rules say they must be fresh every day and house-keeping forgot, sir. So sorry, sir.'

Great God, was I to have no peace, even here? Had I

not suffered sufficiently for one day? My scratched face and aching knees from my enforced flight were pain enough, without further aggravation. Better perhaps to permit the wretched woman to complete her task and be done with it. I marked the page and set aside my reading matter: an old copy of *The Police Gazette* that I had been perusing in my quest for inspiration, and went to the door. Through the spy-hole, all I was able to see was a lace-trimmed cap surmounting a pile of towels. The face behind it was not visible.

'Who are you?'

'Lottie, sir: Charlotte West that is, from house-keeping, sir, begging your pardon for the intrusion, sir.'

'Oh, very well.' I opened the door before returning to the chair and resuming my reading. The maid bustled in behind me and went into the bathroom. 'Just do your job and be gone. I shall be making a complaint to my Great-Uncle Ezekiel, Lord Grosvenor, personally, about such poor service.' I returned my attention to the newspaper – a diverting narration of an undertaker, who created his own customers, being hanged at Birmingham Gaol. 'And these constant interruptions are not to be borne!'

'You won't have to bear them, Mr Grosvenor-Berkeley,' said a voice I recognised. 'They don't bother much with changing the towels in Newgate.'

'Ex-Inspector Sutton! Of all the impertinence...'

I flung the *Gazette* at him and leapt from my chair while Sutton was fighting to extricate himself from a cascade of newsprint. I made for the door but found an avalanche of towels falling upon me. I tripped and went down. Before I could rise again, a weight fell on my back, towels smothered me and enveloped my head, so I feared I might suffocate.

'Unhand me, you wastrel,' I cried, but my words were muffled. I felt my arms being pulled behind me and secured before the towels were removed and I was assisted up off the carpet.

'I arrest you in the name of the law, sir,' Sutton announced, his authority considerably diminished by the fact that one hand clutched desperately at the waistband of his trousers. He had employed his braces to bind my wrists – the image was quite laughable and I surrendered to considerable mirth. 'Don't know what you find funny in this matter,' he said, 'You won't be laughing in front of the magistrate in the morning. And that's just the beginning. It's Newgate and the Old Bailey for you.' Sutton turned to the maid: 'Nell, go fetch Constable Michaelson. He should be in the vestibule or just outside.'

I might have known: she was no maid but that hussy of a wife of his. I had become careless, permitting her to enter my suite without confirming her credentials. But perhaps all was not lost. My hands might be tied, but I still had the use of my elbows and feet. With the slut departed, I was alone with Sutton. As he attempted to manoeuvre me towards the armchair, before he could force me to be seated and at a disadvantage, I elbowed him in the solar plexus. He gasped and fell to his knees, wheezing, and I made my escape through the open door.

No, not that procrastinating lift contraption. That was too slow. The policeman and that wretched female would come by such means, no doubt. I fled down the stairs as precipitously as maybe. Having my hands restrained did nothing to assist. I was descending from the second to the first floor when I espied something dark in colour spread across the next stair. Unable to arrest my flight, I did my utmost to avoid it, but I was unbalanced. I could not save myself. Even as I was in mid-air, awaiting the inevitable catastrophic impact, I recognised that deadly feline as the cause of my undoing.

CHAPTER 21

Friday, 26th October
The Grosvenor-Berkeley residence,
Primrose Hill

NATHANIEL GROSVENOR-BERKELEY, Lord Heaton of Heaton-Magna, was currently detained in a nice, comfortable cell in the bowels of Scotland Yard. Blue blood and an impeccable pedigree could not divert the due process of the law. At least, Albert fervently hoped they couldn't. The trouble was, Grosvenor-Berkeley was well acquainted with a good many people in very high places, not least *Those Upstairs*. A hefty bandage around the prisoner's head and his insistence that he had no recollection of anything, even his own name, weren't helping the Metropolitan Police in their attempts to build a cast-iron case against him, either.

However, a warrant to conduct a search of his lordship's residence at Primrose Hill had been obtained. Under strict instructions from Chief Constable Williamson, Albert, though still on suspension, was permitted to 'observe' the procedure but in no way to touch anything or hinder the search. His presence was only permitted because it seemed the grand house was the most likely place to which his wife had been taken, by force, following her abduction.

'Yes,' Albert said, 'This room certainly fits Nell's description of the library to which she was brought. The French windows, the apple tree and wall beyond... yes, I think this is the place. It all tallies with the story of her escape.'

Inspector Abberline nodded.

'If we can find the chest in which she was transported, that would help. Look around, Sutton, but remember, don't touch anything. Just tell one of the sergeants or constables.' Abberline seated himself in a deep leather chair behind a large mahogany table, looking quite at home, pulling out drawers and swamping the top with papers to be sorted through.

Albert wandered around the bookshelves, not sure what he was looking for. Every volume was bound in matching dark Moroccan leather with gilt lettering and a coat-of-arms: atlases, history books, poetry, entomology, geology, railway timetables and legal books, even a few sensational novels but nothing incriminating. Of a sudden, he gasped. He had seen that gilded coat-of-arms before. He remembered seeing it emblazoned on the carriage that had run him down in the fog that evening and, perhaps, adorning the doors of the vehicle turning outside *Bennett's*. The monster must have been shadowing his every move for weeks! But why? What had he ever done to offend Grosvenor-Berkeley? What could warrant such a vindictive vendetta against him? The mystery deepened, as if it wasn't dark and sordid enough.

Shaking his head over the matter, Albert moved on to the next room, a withdrawing room. An elaborate

Addams overmantle made a fine centrepiece. An incredibly large chandelier seemed to be defying gravity, that such a weight of fine crystal did not bring down the plasterwork ceiling from which it was suspended. Albert found such opulence a little intimidating, feeling he ought to doff his cap, as he would in church. The sheen on the Chinese silk wallpaper made it seem like polished sapphire. How much did such splendour cost per yard, he wondered and, just out of interest, paced the length of the wall. That was odd. He must have miscounted. He repeated the process. No. Definitely a little under eight yards.

Frowning, he returned to the library and paced out the wall adjoining the withdrawing room next door. Even allowing for the depth of the bookshelves, almost six feet were missing from the length of the library.

'Inspector Abberline? I think I may have found something,' Albert said. Abberline was busy trying to shove papers back into a drawer in such disarray that they wouldn't fit.

'You were ordered not to touch anything, Sutton,' Abberline growled, using brute force to ram the drawer closed.

'I didn't. It's just that this library isn't big enough.'

'Big enough to hold a bloody dance! What do you mean, it's not big enough?'

'This room is at the corner of the house, yes?'

Abberline nodded.

'So, the French windows form one outside wall and those bookshelves are against another outside wall. You agree?'

'We don't have time for games...'

'Bear with me, please. Now, when we walked around the outside of the house, you recall that this end wall, behind the books, was flush with the wall of the room next door? It's solid brick, no windows because it's north-facing, to retain heat.'

'I'm not a bloody architect. Get on with it.'

'Then why is it, with both outer walls and internal doorways level with each other in the two rooms, the library is at least two paces shorter in length than the withdrawing room?'

'I don't know, Sutton, you've lost me. And why does it matter, anyway? We're not here to measure up for new floor runners. Now get out and go pester Sergeant Hobhouse or someone.'

Abberline returned to the table to shuffle more paper.

'But don't you see, Fred?' Albert insisted, forgetting courtesy and leaning across the table, 'There must be a secret room behind the shelves to use up the remaining six feet or so of length.'

'Secret room! Don't be preposterous. You've been reading too many *Penny Dreadfuls*, you have.'

'No. I'm certain of it. Measure it out yourself, if you don't believe me.'

Abberline heaved a sigh.

'Very well. But if this turns out to be a waste of time... Sergeant Hobhouse!'

Fortunately for Albert, half an hour later, after a lengthy, unproductive search for a tape measure, or even a ball of string, the sergeant's repeated pacing out confirmed there were, indeed, a couple of yards of space unaccounted for in the library.

'Now to find a way in,' said Albert, his persistence having been rewarded.

Abberline tutted.

'I suppose, as in the best melodramas, there must be some ingenious mechanical device secreted in amongst the books which opens a concealed door. This could take hours,' he muttered.

But already, Albert and Sergeant Hobhouse had been

joined by Constable Michaelson in removing books from the shelves.

'Careful with them, constable,' Abberline warned, seeing Michaelson sweeping up a hefty pile of volumes in his arms before dumping them in a heap on the Turkey carpet. 'We don't want his lordship – or his heirs, come to that – suing the Met for damaging his property. Those books look expensive.'

It took the three men, jacketless, close to an hour, bearing in mind Abberline's warning, to clear the shelves all along the back wall, stacking the books on the floor by the French windows. There was no sign of a knob, a bell pull, a lever or handle that might operate a mechanism to open a door. Nor was there any evidence of a secret panel or hinges.

Albert mopped his brow on his handkerchief and sighed. He'd been so certain.

Hobhouse leaned against the table, red in the face, shirt sleeves rolled above the elbow.

'Well? Now what... sir?' he asked, adding the polite address as an afterthought, frowning at Albert. 'I s'pose you expect us to put all them damned books back agen?'

Michaelson was sitting cross-legged like an Indian fakir on the floor, toying with the fringe on the carpet.

'I reckon it's got to be easier than this, Mr Sutton, sir. His lordship don't look to me to be the type to go shiftin' books t' get into his secret lair every time. Too idle fer that.'

'If there *is* a secret lair in the first place, constable,' said Abberline. 'In the meantime, I'm due to report to the Chief Constable after he's had his dinner – I beg his pardon: luncheon – so I'll leave you to it.' He heaved himself out of the depths of the leather chair. 'Keep me informed of developments, Sutton. I'll want a written report on my desk first thing in the morning.' Then he left.

'Of course, sir.' Albert felt his heart flip. Did that mean

he was no longer on suspension? Or had Abberline simply forgotten that was the case? No, he decided. Only the Chief Constable could reinstate him and return his warrant card but, at least, there might be a glimmer of hope now. And if he found damning evidence of Grosvenor-Berkeley's guilt in a secret room, that could only improve things, couldn't it? 'Come along, lads, we can't give up now,' he said. 'It's here somewhere, I know it is.'

Hobhouse's dour look said more than words ever could, but young Michaelson got to his feet in a single agile movement – much envied by Albert – keen to continue the search. As the constable stood on the Turkey carpet, Albert heard something.

'What was that? Did you hear that squeak, constable?'

'Mouse, I expect, sir.'

'No. Lift the carpet. Come, give me a hand, here.'

Just beneath the edge of the fine carpet, where Michaelson had been sitting, a six-inch section of polished floorboard with a knothole in it was, quite clearly, cut out from the rest of the board. Sutton's knelt down and found that his finger fitted into the knothole perfectly. He lifted the section of board away and beneath was a brass handle of the kind often attached to a substantial drawer. He lifted it. Nothing. Pulled it. Again, nothing. Then he turned it.

With a near inaudible click, an entire section of bookshelves in the centre of the back wall moved, swinging open a few inches. Michaelson cheered; Hobhouse grunted; Albert felt relieved – and a little smug. So relieved, in fact, that he forgot to be embarrassed when his knee cracked loudly as he got up off the floor.

Albert opened wide the secret door and peered in. Such were the modern conveniences of the house, there was even a switch on the wall inside for an electrical light. Albert had seen switches before but never had cause to use one. He did so now, half prepared for a terrible shock, even an explosion. He need not have feared. The only shock was the incredible brightness of the illumination from the single glass globe suspended at the end of its twisted brown cable, like a tiny chandelier dangling from the centre of the ceiling. But there was no time to wonder at such marvels of modern ingenuity. Hobhouse and Michaelson squeezed in behind Albert.

There was a walnut bureau against the wall to the left and a comfortable armchair. Every inch of the remaining wall space was taken up with what appeared to be the glass cabinets and drawers of a private museum.

'Well, I never,' Hobhouse said, 'What a closet of horrors we 'ave 'ere, Mr Sutton.'

'Take care with all this. It's evidence, lads,' Albert reminded them.

He found the bureau was unlocked and lowered the front section to form an escritoire, revealing a row of notebooks and photograph albums. Opening a leather bound album at random, he saw a series of pictures of a large dog, hanging by the neck. In the first image, the subject was blurred, indicating that the unfortunate beast was moving; the second image less so and in the third, the dog must have been motionless for the image was sharp. Beneath, was written the legend: Experiment 1,742B, 21st April 1879, see Journal Book 21, pp.43-45.

Albert shuddered, not just at the photographs but at the numbers neatly written beneath and what they implied. Hundreds, if not thousands, of so-called experiments! And every page he turned displayed images more gruesome than the last.

''Ere, look at these. Ain't they pretty.' Michaelson was standing before a glass aquarium tank. Inside it, a half dozen tiny frogs, bright yellow in colour, hopped about.

Hobhouse grunted.

'Leave 'em be,' he ordered. 'Evidence.'

Albert found a white envelope pushed into one of the little cubbyholes at the back of the bureau. He took it out, hoping it would prove to be something less ghastly. It was sealed but held something circular and quite bulky. He would hazard a guess that it contained a pocket watch, by the feel of it, but what came as a real surprise was the name of the addressee: Chief Constable Adolphus Williamson.

Of a sudden, Constable Michaelson, who had been looking along the shelves, dropped a sealed jar, gasped and fled. The stench of formaldehyde from the smashed jar, familiar from St Thomas's mortuary, filled the space, making their eyes water and setting both Albert and Hobhouse coughing. Through his tears, Albert looked down, intending to avoid the shards of glass. No wonder the young constable had fled. There, upon the floor in a puddle of preserving fluid and shattered glass lay a tiny unborn baby, its umbilical cord still attached and trailing. A closet of horrors, indeed.

CHAPTER 22

Monday, 29ᵗʰ October

'NO, THE devil isn't dead, Nell. His head must be as hard as a marble slab. St Thomas's say he has a concussion, but he will live.' Albert and Nell were sipping tea in Mrs Mumble's tea shop, a plate of Cheddar cheese and onion scones, fresh from the oven, sat on the table between them, filling the air with their delicious savoury steam.

Nell helped herself to a scone, halved it neatly, then smeared it with a generous knife full of butter and strawberry jam. The butter was already melting and dripping before she took a bite.

Albert couldn't understand why his wife had lately taken to smothering everything in jam.

'I'm not sure whether to be pleased he survived.' Nell mopped a dribble of butter from her chin with a gingham napkin. I suppose it means he will have to stand trial, at least. I hope they hang him. The clumsy oaf almost crushed poor Blackstock.'

'He did a great deal worse than that,' Albert explained as he refilled the teacups, staring and wondering at Nell as she piled more jam on the cheese and onion scone. 'His home was full of gruesome souvenirs and an entire catalogue of his murdering escapades.'

Nell mopped up the crumbs and wiped her lips.

'How many did he kill?'

'At least two dozen human victims by every conceivable means: poisoning, stabbing, strangling, shooting... you name it, he tried it as his *modus operandi* at some point. If his records are to be believed, he began by killing his brother when they were children, and later his mother. The list is horrendous.'

'But at least they found out who really stole the Ripper case notes. At least you're re-instated now.'

'Yes. The cloud has been lifted from my life... our lives.' Albert sat in silence for a moment. He had decided Nell should never learn the full story as revealed in Grosvenor-Berkeley's journal: how he had spent weeks trying to goad him to the point of suicide by ruining his career, his marriage and everything he held dear.

'Will I have to appear in court at his trial?' Nell asked, 'What do they say? Testify? That sounds quite important, doesn't it?

'I'm afraid, Nell, there is some doubt about the case ever coming to trial.'

'Why? How can that be? He's as guilty as Satan.'

'I know, but justice can only be served on those in full command of their senses, in their right mind.'

'You mean he's insane, so they'll let him off? That can't be right. It can't be, Albert. It's not fair!' Nell held her napkin to her eyes. 'It's just not fair if he gets away with his terrible crimes... not us alone but all the other poor people...'

Albert took his wife's hand in his as tears dripped onto her plate:

'That is true, but you see the doctors say he has lost his memory; he has amnesia, as they call it. He can't remember committing any of those murders. He doesn't even recognise his own name, so he cannot plead... cannot declare himself guilty or otherwise.'

'And you believe that?' Nell was frowning. 'He's a villain, an arch-liar and the police believe him?'

'We have no choice, Nell. It's what the doctors say... what the law determines... a man with no memory cannot stand trial, no matter how much evidence there is against him.'

'Then I wish he'd died when he fell down the stairs at the hotel. He doesn't deserve to live.'

'Have another scone, dearest,' Albert said in a soothing tone, putting one on her plate and passing the dish of jam.

'I'm not hungry anymore. How can I be, knowing he's got off so lightly?' She pushed her plate aside.

'You cannot starve yourself because of him, sweetheart. For one thing, that would please him very much, if he knew. Besides, it is possible, apparently, to recover from amnesia.'

Nell's eyes brightened and she pulled the plate towards her, attacking the next scone dextrously.

'Then I have never wished so heartily for the recovery of a man so loathsome.' She drained her teacup and tested the pot. 'Another pot of tea, if you please, Mrs Mumbles. We are celebrating this afternoon.' She turned back to Albert. 'Besides, I have something to say to you. I couldn't tell you before, or you'd never have let me join the chase and with you out of a job, it didn't seem the right time to tell you there will soon be another mouth...'

Nell never finished the sentence because Albert's lips were pressed fervently against hers, crumbs and all, his eyes bright with joy.

'Oh, Nell, what wonderful news, sweetheart.' No villain could spoil this moment, could he? 'When?'

'The beginning of summer; around bluebell time, I think.'

The kiss had smudged jam on Nell's lips and Albert fished in his jacket pocket for a handkerchief to wipe her smiling mouth. Along with the handkerchief, he found the envelope from Primrose Hill, the one addressed to the Chief Constable. He had pocketed and forgotten it when Constable Michaelson dropped the specimen jar and they'd all fled the fumes of formaldehyde. He ought to deliver it, however belatedly. All weekend it had sat in his jacket pocket, but it might be important to the case.

CHAPTER 23

Tuesday, 30th October
Scotland Yard

'**C**HIEF CONSTABLE,** sir,' Albert spoke politely as he encountered Williamson in the corridor as he was leaving his office, 'If I might have a moment of your time, please?'

'You're officially back on duty, Sutton. Be grateful for that, can't you? What more do you want, damn it? I'm a busy man.'

'Forgive me, sir, but I found this on Friday, while we were searching the Primrose Hill house. I haven't had the opportunity before to give it to you in person. I thought that best, rather than keep it as evidence.' Albert handed the Chief Constable the envelope addressed to him, the name written in Grosvenor-Berkeley's hand.

'What is it?'

'I don't know, sir, I haven't opened it. I would say it feels like a pocket watch but...'

Williamson had already torn open the envelope. He emptied the contents into the palm of his hand. It was, indeed, a watch. A fine piece in a silver case. There was also a single sheet of paper. The Chief Constable staggered slightly and leaned against the wall.

'Sir? Are you unwell, sir?'

Albert took a hold of his superior's arm. The man had paled alarmingly to the hue of uncooked pastry behind his beard. Albert guided him back into his office and lowered him into the chair behind the desk.

'I'll have Michaelson fetch you some tea, shall I, sir? An ideal restorative: hot and sweet.'

'Bloody tea, be damned. There's brandy in that drawer...'

Albert found the brandy and a glass; poured a generous measure and set it on the desk. Williamson drank it down in one go.

'Another!'

'Yes, sir.' As he refilled the glass, Albert caught a glimpse of the sheet of paper from the envelope. The Chief Constable's hand was shaking as he held it but not so much that Albert couldn't read what it said, for the letters were large and bold: SAUCY JACK WON'T BE NEEDING THIS ANYMORE. The watch lay face down upon the empty envelope on the desk. It was more difficult to read the copperplate inscription etched on the silver, but it too was legible, just: *To Thomas, on your coming of age, from Uncle Dolly.*

Albert almost dropped the brandy bottle in shock but succeeded in withholding his exclamation of surprise. Could this be? No, of course it couldn't. It was all lies. Another of Grosvenor-Berkeley's horrible schemes, designed to cause the greatest distress possible. If any real name could be put to Jack the Ripper, it was most likely Grosvenor-Berkeley's own. This fellow, Thomas, might well be just another of his many unfortunate victims. But how many 'Uncle Dollies' could there be?

'Leave me, Sutton. Tell the desk sergeant I am not to be disturbed under any circumstances. I don't care if the Prince of Wales visits and the bloody place is on fire. Understand?'

'Of course, sir.' Albert left the brandy bottle beside the glass on the desk and left Williamson to his solitary brooding.

~

Downstairs, at his own desk once more, Albert should have felt at ease, except that he was faced with the notebooks, sketchbooks and photograph albums from Primrose Hill. Thank God, the specimen jars had been boxed and transported to the mortuary at St Thomas's, though what would be done with them, nobody was sure. Grosvenor-Berkeley was both organised and detailed in everything he recorded. To be honest, the minutiae of his murderous endeavours were far more than Albert ever wanted to know, but duty required him to look at and read everything. By eleven o'clock, he had to take a rest from the horrors.

'Michaelson! Fetch me a cup of tea will you, please?'

'And a scone... or two, Mr Sutton?' the constable suggested, grinning.

'Good Lord, no. My stomach cannot withstand food. Have you seen what is in these books? I shall not be able to eat for a month after this.'

'Tea it is then.' The constable went off, looking disappointed. Albert realised, belatedly, the young man had probably hoped to share a scone, as once before. He shoved aside a particularly gruesome series of photographs that he could no longer bear to contemplate and picked up a notebook at random. The cover was inscribed *August*

1888 – obviously the most recent and not completely full, thankfully. A thought struck him and he leafed through the pages. He seemed to recall a woman, well dressed and accompanied by a little dog he'd been required to catch, visiting the Chief Constable, trying to persuade him to search for her missing nephew. She'd called Williamson 'Dolly'. If she was a relative of Williamson, then might they have been talking about 'Thomas', the owner of that fine watch?

Albert found it. Dated Saturday 29th September. There, recorded in scrupulous detail, was Grosvenor-Berkeley's encounter with Thomas Williamson. The young man's appearance was so precisely described that Albert realised he had visited his uncle here, at the Yard, on three or four occasions. They had even been introduced, although Albert had always had more pressing matters on his mind and had quite forgotten the man – until now. Reading on, he first assumed that Grosvenor-Berkeley singled him out as a victim because he was the Chief Constable's nephew but when he reached the itemised account of what occurred in Dutfield's Yard off Berner Street, Albert couldn't help gasping aloud.

'You alright, Mr Sutton, sir?' Michaelson asked as he came in with a covered tray from the tea shop across the road. 'You look like I got this just in time. Shall I play muvver, then?'

'Er.' Albert hastily closed the notebook and set it aside. He cleared his throat and wiped his sweaty palms on his trousers beneath the desk. 'Yes, constable. I should be much obliged if you would.' Obliged indeed, for he feared his hands would be shaking noticeably if he poured it himself. Strong tea cascaded from the spout of the blue-flowered teapot, through the strainer and into the matching cup. The fragrant steam was enough to bring Albert back from the world of horrors that lay, awaiting revelation, in those neatly written pages. He added milk and four sugar cubes to the cup and stirred it forcibly with the teaspoon for some little while.

'I reckon Mrs Mumbles'll still be wantin' some pattern left on that cup, sir, when yer finished?'

'What?'

'Stirrin' yer tea, Mr Sutton.'

'Oh, yes. Thank you, constable.'

There was enough tea in the pot for two cups at least. Michaelson sniffed as he closed the door. He wouldn't have minded fetching his own old enamel cup to share. Mr Sutton was in an odd mood today when you'd think he'd be overjoyed at solving the Grosvenor-Berkeley case and being reinstated.

Albert sipped his tea, sighing as he felt his taut nerves easing under the influence of the hot, sugary brew. Tea: the best medicine known to man. Somewhat restored, reluctant but nevertheless intrigued, he returned to his reading. *You call yourself Jack the Ripper!* The words leapt from the page. Stunned, Albert read the passage again. Grosvenor-Berkeley was accusing Thomas Williamson of being the notorious murderer of women in Whitechapel. That could not be true, surely. The Chief Constable's own nephew? Absurd. Of course it wasn't true. Was it?

The rest of the tea grew cold while Albert went through the entry for that Saturday night in September last, over and over. He came to realise that Grosvenor-Berkeley had merely suspected what sort of fellow Saucy Jack might be with no more idea that it would be Williamson's nephew than anyone else. In fact, Grosvenor-Berkeley had proved himself a most accomplished detective, achieving what nobody at the Yard could manage to do.

No. Albert refused to believe it. This was just Grosvenor-Berkeley's warped fantasy, invented for his own deviant pleasure. Such a man's writings were not to be taken as a truthful account by any means. A sordid collection of lies, that's what it was: all lies.

Albert moved on to more recent entries and discovered his own name mentioned. His collision with the brougham in the fog – Grosvenor-Berkeley had indeed been the driver of the vehicle. The time and place of the incident were accurately noted. So too was Nell's abduction and the removal of the Ripper file, money and jewellery from the cupboard in this very office. Albert leaned back in his chair, scrubbing his face with his hands, as if to scour away this awful knowledge. Fully detailed in neat script was the payment made to a prostitute, Maudie Cooper, for visiting Summerlea Villas. Another had been made to Hobbs and Martin to harass the same address in the guise of bailiffs.

Noted also was the purpose behind all these occurrences: Grosvenor-Berkeley had intended to drive him to the brink of despair, hoping to be present when he – Albert Sutton – reached the point where he could withstand no more torment and resorted to ending his own life! He wondered if he would ever have reached such a point. If he had lost Nell, his job, his house, his reputation... everything he held dear, well then, possibly, Grosvenor-Berkeley might just have got his wish.

Albert laughed humourlessly at a list of ways and means he might have chosen to end it all, noted down on the next page. Grosvenor-Berkeley had thought throwing himself in front of a locomotive on the railway the most likely. Drowning in the Thames and slitting his wrists were second and third upon the list. Wrong, wrong, wrong. Grosvenor-Berkeley did not know of the revolver in his chest of drawers. A Beaumont-Adams double-action piece made by Robert Adams of London, it had been his father's, used in anger in India thirty years ago. Harry Sutton had worked for the Honourable East India Company and fought at Lucknow during the Mutiny of 1857 – a hero by all accounts. Albert still cleaned and oiled the weapon regularly, in his father's memory, so it was perfectly serviceable, devastating at thirty-five yards, and he knew how to use it. With no other choice, he would have put it to his head and – since it was self-cocking – simply pulled the trigger. Messy but quick. In fact, if he'd known sooner what that devil was up to, he'd have used the revolver before now, to put an end to the perpetrator of so much misery. Even with the rogue in custody, the idea certainly had its appeal.

The immediate question, however, was what to do about the identification of the Chief Constable's nephew, not only as one of Grosvenor-Berkeley's victims but as the Whitechapel killer? Albert was in two minds. He could neatly remove those pages from the notebook, telling of Jack the Ripper's identity, whether or not they were true, and spare Williamson's family any further grief. Although, in this case, Whitechapel would continue to fear the possibility of more murders, not knowing Saucy Jack was gone. Or he could give the offending book to Williamson and let the Chief Constable decide what he did with the information. In light of his own recent suspension, the second option was by far the most sensible, rather than taking the matter into his own hands.

With heavy tread, Albert climbed the stairs to his superior's office, feeling saddened at the action he was about to take. Williamson had already suffered the appalling shock of his nephew's murder, now a whole cruet's worth of salt was going to be rubbed into the open wound of grief. At the door, his hand raised to knock, he changed his mind, unable to inflict more pain. But then the door opened as Fred Abberline came out and the Chief Constable caught sight of Albert in the doorway.

'Oh, just the fellow. Come in, Sutton, I have a job for you. Abberline tells me the exhibits taken to St Thomas's have yet to be inventoried. You're just the man...'

Albert put the notebook on Williamson's desk and slid it across the highly polished wood.

'I apologise, sir, but before I do anything more in this case, I think you ought to read some of the entries in this book. It may make a difference as to how we, er, continue with the investigation. Page twenty-seven, sir...'

The two men exchanged looks. Sutton's sombre expression told Williamson he wouldn't like what he read; Albert could see his superior was fearful of what he might learn. There was no way he could soften the blow.

If it was possible for a human being to crumble, splinter and fall apart, that was what Albert witnessed in that office, across the desk. The Chief Constable appeared to shrink inside his uniform, his complexion turning grey, his body trembling. Eventually, he waved Albert away, unable even to speak to dismiss him. Uncertain what to do for the best, Albert was slow to descend the stair. He was only a half dozen steps down when the deafening report of a gunshot assailed his ears. He turned and ran back to the office, flinging the door wide. He did not enter. There was no point.

Sergeant Hobhouse and Constable Michaelson were first up the stairs, followed swiftly by Inspector Abbeline and anyone else close enough to have heard the shot. Williamson lay sprawled across his desk, a Navy-issue Colt still smoking in his right hand. Blood pooled crimson beneath his head, soaking into the notebook, causing the ink to run, obliterating the words forever. It was a decision, of sorts, and Grosvenor-Berkeley had achieved his suicide victim, just not the one he'd planned.

Albert felt the wetness of tears on his cheek and the weight of guilt in his heart but what else could he have done?

CHAPTER 24

Wednesday, 31st October

NELL LOOKED at her husband's breakfast plate, untouched.

'I know I'm not much of a cook, Albert, but surely my bacon and eggs aren't as bad as that? You didn't eat so much as a morsel of the supper I made especially for you last evening, either. And I thought kidney pudding was your favourite. Please eat the bread and butter, at least.' She nudged his foot beneath the table. She did not know her husband would probably never be able to eat kidney again, not with the memory of that horror, wrapped in an enamelled box and delivered to Inspector Abberline not so long ago, still engraved in his mind. And all those other body parts preserved in jars... It was enough to force a man to live on fruit and vegetables forever. And now Williamson's death...

'What, Nell? What were you saying?' Albert stopped staring at the wall above the range.

'Eat something, won't you?'

'I'm not hungry. Sorry.'

'No need to lie to me, Albert. If my cooking is inedible, then say so.'

'I'm sure it's fine, Nell. I just can't...'

'Are you ill? Do you need a doctor?'

'Please don't fuss me. I'm not ill.' He left the table so suddenly, he jarred the teacups, spilling the tea he hadn't touched. 'I'll be late at the Yard at this rate.'

'But it's hardly eight o'clock...' Nell's protest was made to her husband's departing back as he left, still buttoning his coat on a cold, drizzly morning. 'Oh, well, Blackstock, more food for you then, though it seems such a waste.' The cat simply showed his appreciation by wolfing down the bacon and eggs, while Nell drank the tea and ate the bread and butter before the crusts should begin to curl. She couldn't face a fried breakfast either and with good reason. She wondered why Albert couldn't. He had been so distracted since he came home last eve. Something had occurred but what might it be?

The Old Bailey

Albert did not go to the Yard as usual this morning. Instead, his destination was the Old Bailey where a judge was to determine whether Nathaniel Grosvenor-Berkeley, Lord Heaton of Heaton-Magna, was fit to plead and stand trial for his innumerable crimes.

Mr Justice McLaughlin QC was a reasonable choice, despite his unctuous smile and appalling halitosis. Stern but fair, at least he wasn't a member of the aristocracy and therefore, perhaps inclined to have sympathy with a fellow peer of the realm. To Albert's mind, the accused deserved the ultimate punishment at the earliest opportunity –

dangling at the end of a rope – and not a single shred of sympathy from anyone.

❧

My head was very sore, as though I had consumed an entire bottle of Armagnac. That much at least required no pretence. As for my other symptoms? You well know by now, dear reader, of my consummate skill as an actor. Faltering steps, a vague expression of bewilderment and unfocused eyes were all perfectly within my capacity to demonstrate with very little inconvenience to my person. To compound my supposed lack of wits, I gave no hint of recognition when they addressed me by name and their numerous inquisitions gained not a solitary meaningful reply. The fools were only too eager to attribute my lack of response to a severe case of traumatic amnesia, due to the head injury I had sustained upon the hotel staircase. I was more than content to permit such a conclusion and did nothing to cause them to reconsider their error in diagnosis. I had an unpleasant headache, a small cut above my right eye that had necessitated two sutures and a contusion the size and shape of a quail's egg in the same vicinity. Those matters aside, my symptoms were entirely fictitious.

I was transported from St Thomas's Hospital in an enclosed coach that stank of other people's sweat and bodily fluids. Though utterly revolted by the stench, I feigned not to notice. My hands lay limp in my lap, cuffed, not that such primitive shackles would prove a problem if I wished them removed. A lady's hatpin – such items had numerous uses, as I'm sure you have realised before now – lay inserted behind my lapel and it would have required but a few moments of sleight-of-hand to obtain my release. I was accompanied by the police surgeon, a Dr Philips, a nonentity in a most out-dated jacket that did him no favours, its bold greenish-yellow check serving to enhance his unhealthy florid complexion and faded reddish mutton-chop whiskers. Sitting opposite us in the coach were two policemen from H division, Stepney and Whitechapel: a sergeant with a grotesquely misshapen nose and the rough complexion of a ploughman and a constable who looked but lately to have left his rudimentary school ABC book. I leaned back upon the uncushioned wooden seat and closed my eyes for the duration of the journey to the Old Bailey. This posture spared me the unpleasant sight of those sitting in such close proximity and assisted the illusion that I was quite enfeebled and unwell. I would bide my time.

~

Albert fidgeted, worrying at his thumbnail as he sat upon the hard chair, awaiting the arrival of the defendant. What was keeping them? He had already been called to the dock. Ah! A door creaked down below; boots came up the wooden stairs – slowly. Albert was shocked when Grosvenor-Berkeley appeared at last, leaning heavily on the two policemen, one at either elbow. It seemed as though, without their stalwart support, he might collapse in a heap behind the carved balustrade around the dock. Was this truly the same devil who had committed countless ghastly crimes? He looked so helpless and pathetic now, it hardly seemed credible. Albert chewed his nail again, wondering what impression Grosvenor-Berkeley would make upon the judge.

Mr Justice McLaughlin peered over his pince-nez at the accused. He had read the case notes last evening and, whatever sort of fellow he had expected to appear before him this morning, it wasn't this sorry-looking individual, slumped on the stool.

'The prisoner will stand,' announced the clerk of the court.

Grosvenor-Berkeley did not move; his eyes unfocused, his face expressionless.

'The prisoner will stand,' repeated the clerk.

The police sergeant tried to haul the prisoner to his feet, but he was a dead weight. The skinny young constable did his best to assist.

'Stand up, you bugger,' the sergeant growled, to no effect whatsoever.

'That will do, sergeant,' the judge said, tut-tutting at the use of 'language' in his court. 'The prisoner may remain seated if he is unable to stand.'

The policemen dropped Grosvenor-Berkeley back onto the stool like a sack of wet potatoes where he sat, staring blankly at nothing as before.

'Is he able to state his name, as required?'

The clerk conferred for a few moments with the sergeant and with Dr Philips who had hastened forward with a phial of *sal volatile,* hoping to rouse the prisoner to some degree.

'I fear not, your honour,' the clerk said.

'Most irregular. The fellow should not have been taken from his bed. Is there a medical report?'

'Yes, your honour. Two, actually. One from Dr Philips, who is present in court, regarding the prisoner's physical injuries, and another written by a Dr Mansfield, detailing the prisoner's state of mind. Dr Mansfield is a consultant at both Bedlam Hospital and Broadmore Mental Institution, specialising in the study of the criminally insane. He will be available as an expert witness, to testify at the trial, if required.'

The judge removed his pince-nez, polished the lenses on the fur cuff of his robe, replaced them and took the manila folders from the clerk.

Albert was chewing at his thumbnail again, watching as McLaughlin read the reports. The judge studied them, going back and forth through the pages, re-reading some passages. He paused at one point to ask Dr Philips for further clarification concerning the defendant's head injury, then continued his perusal. It seemed to Albert that the judge was taking far too long to read the slim reports. Was he deliberately delaying his decision as to whether the accused was fit to plead?

'Well, yes, indeed...' The judge tidied the papers, slipped them back inside the manila folders and cleared his throat. 'Ahem. It seems to me that the accused is quite unfit to plead, being mentally incapacitated...'

Albert groaned. The devil was going to get away with it!

'For the present,' McLaughlin continued. 'This hearing will be resumed in twenty-eight days, pending the recovery of the accused, or at least his improved state of health. Thank you.'

So that was that. At least for now. Albert discovered his thumb was bloodied, the nail chewed to the quick. He hadn't realised he was in so nervous a state. Williamson's death had also upset him deeply and now he had the inquest to attend. The Lord knew he was in dire need of a cup of Mrs Mumbles' strong tea back in Westminster.

CHAPTER 25

Friday, 9th November – nine days later
St Thomas's Hospital

SUCH FOOLS! How easy it is to convince them that I remember nothing at all, not even my own name. As if I could forget that I am a Grosvenor-Berkeley. That is not to say that the injury to my head was negligible. Indeed, for four days, the pain was so considerable and distracting, coherent thought had proved difficult even for me. Yet I turned such a disadvantage into an advantage and was able to convince them of my supposed amnesiac condition quite easily.

I have now lain supine in St Thomas's Infirmary for an entire week or more, upon the instruction of some useless physician that bed rest is the most appropriate treatment for my mental state. Idiot! Does he truly suppose that being confined amongst such types as he refers to as 'patients' – out of work dockers and railway navvies, for the most part, afflicted with broken bones, running sores and a plethora of

vile ailments that cause such a stench as is not to be borne
– will aid one's recovery?

I have no intention of staying here and will depart as
soon as circumstance allows. By 'circumstance' I refer to the
police constable who sits ever at the foot of my bed. His
identity changes every eight hours in rotation. There is the
fat fellow of middle years who must fancy himself quite the
Lothario and eyes up the nurses. He arrives at ten o'clock
each evening, makes lewd comments to the younger nurses
and settles down to snore away the night hours before being
brought tea at six in the morning and departing hence. His
place is then occupied by the young one, he with no more
substance to him than a wisp of Thames mist, gawky and
spotty, having as much intelligence as a potted aspidistra.
He makes himself scarce during the consultant's rounds but
returns promptly afterwards to resume his watch.

And then there is Constable Michaelson who actually
assisted in my apprehension, I believe. He arrives during
luncheon – if the pig-swill they serve here can ever be
thus described – which is brought in at a quarter to two
o'clock. I intend to repay Michaelson in due course for
his temerity and have it in mind that, if at all possible, my
escape from this damned place shall be expedited upon
his watch. He will be the one to suffer the consequences.
In determining this, I have set myself a more daunting
challenge than might otherwise have been the case. Either
of the other two constables would be easier to dupe, to
confound with a little obfuscation, while Michaelson has a
modicum of reason, even perception. But when have I ever
shirked a challenge and I have nothing else to occupy my
vast intellect as I lie here?

This morning, I had at last been deemed sufficiently
able to make use of one of the communal lavatories. Such
a hateful necessity but at least the staff see to it that each
cubicle is scoured spotlessly clean and the avoidance of

that most humiliating connivance – the bed-pan – was welcome indeed. I took my time in the desirable privacy of the little room, knowing the young constable stood guard beyond the door. I surmised that the convenience had been installed such that it could have accommodated a patient in a bath-chair and two attendants, if required, since it was quite capacious. I examined the small window high up beside the cistern. It could be opened and I balanced upon the wooden lavatory seat to determine whether I could reach it and climb out. Reaching it was not difficult but, having done so, I looked down and discovered that the ward occupied the third floor – a fact of which I had been previously unaware. It was too high to risk escape by such means and, since it backed onto a courtyard within the hospital, surrounded by other buildings, neither was it advantageous as a route to exit the place.

Michaelson would arrive at two o'clock and the unimaginably tedious hour of visiting commenced at three. Sixty ghastly minutes of torture as a parade of mostly women, all of them down-at-heel even in their going-a-visiting hats, trouped in to ask after their loved ones' health, bringing a few wilting flowers and items of ragged night attire, perching on the edge of uncomfortable wooden chairs, poised to flee the instant Matron rang her bell at four. Timing was everything, if I was to effect a successful escape. I would require clothing other than this hideous striped cotton jacket and loose drawstring trousers – pyjamas, they called them – which the hospital has supplied to render one 'decent'. Departing in those, complete with the convenient if disgusting 'drop-seat' at the back which has a button missing, I may as well be wearing prison garb, complete with arrows, for I should be remarked upon at every turn. Not only must I change my clothing but I shall, by some means, have to evade Constable Michaelson's watchful eye.

Observation has always been one secret of my success.

The other is patience. Two days hence, it will be Sunday. The consultant does not do his rounds in the morning; rather, he attends church. Huh! Meanwhile, a minister inflicts his presence upon us here on the ward at midday, carrying out some abysmal canting and chanting, like an African witch-doctor, while the patients feign sleep and the nurses invent urgent matters requiring their immediate attention elsewhere. Last Sunday, he blathered on for precisely an hour and then remained for a further half an hour afterwards, speaking to individuals who would bother to listen and one fellow, whether deluded or merely hypocritical, was eager to have the minister beseech the Lord to grant him a swift recovery. The pair prayed together and much good did it do – a native witch-doctor could likely have done more since the minister was summoned back to give the patient the last rites on Tuesday, just before he died of pneumonia and 'complications'. But the minister might yet have his uses.

Upon this Friday morning, the consultant declared that the bandages about one's head necessitated changing and a young nurse was instructed to perform the task. She brought the appropriate items to the bedside on a small wheeled trolley, like a butler preparatory to serving brandy – which made me realise how long it had been since the last time a decent drink had been provided. The young policeman disappeared for fear of accidentally observing any blood – how he might ever serve his calling with such an aversion quite puzzles me. And indeed, as the nurse unwound the soiled dressings, a deal of dried gore was evident upon the lower layers. The wound must have bled excessively, as head injuries are inclined to do. She then produced a horseshoe-shaped magnet from her pocket and waved it across my head.

'What is the purpose of that?' I enquired, wondering if some new scientific magnetism treatment for head injuries had been invented that had escaped my attention. I read every journal on such matters for one never knows when some novel artifice may come in useful.

'This is my secret, sir,' she whispered. 'I beg you, do not tell, but I once neglected to remove a pin that held a patient's bandages secure. It was lost in his hair. He cried out when it later pricked him and Matron punished me. The magnet makes certain that shan't happen again.'

'You are quite ingenious,' I congratulated her, watching as she put the magnet down on the bed. Upon an instant, I had hidden it within the folds of the threadbare counterpane that passed for bedding in this dismal place. 'Would you be so kind as to fetch me a glass of water as soon as you have finished your task? I should be most grateful for the kindness.'

The silly girl completed her bandaging procedure, gathered up the discarded dressings and tidied the trolley.

'My glass of water,' I reminded her, forcing my mouth to curve in a smile. It would not do for her to think of searching for her magnet until I was able to conceal it adequately. Another expedition to the lavatory would be required. My plan was progressing. How to distract Michaelson's attention when the visitors leave at four o'clock on Sunday was a problem yet to be resolved, but I gave the matter much consideration.

CHAPTER 26

Saturday, 10th November
St Thomas's Hospital

ALBERT DIDN'T like hospitals. Never had. And this particular visit had nothing to recommend it. He could think of more pleasurable occupations for a Saturday morning but consoled himself with the prospect of spending the afternoon with Nell, so long as no other cases developed of a sudden, demanding his presence.

'Good morning, nurse,' he greeted a pretty girl in a trim uniform, removing his new Homburg hat – lately purchased from Jermyn Street to celebrate his reinstatement – and loosening his scarf. It was colder than charity out there and Nell had insisted that he wore her latest efforts at knitting. He wasn't sure that powder blue and sunshine yellow did much for his status as an inspector but if it pleased Nell that was all that mattered. 'I'm Inspector Sutton. I've called to see Mr Berkeley.'

'It isn't visiting time, sir, until three o'clock.'

'This isn't a social call. I'm here to question him on a police matter.'

'Oh. I'll have to ask Matron. Won't you take a seat over there in the waiting area?'

Albert smiled and nodded. Then, he sat for what seemed like an hour at least – although the large clock on the wall disagreed, its pendulum rhythm insisting it was but five-and-twenty minutes – admiring the gleaming linoleum from the most uncomfortable wooden chair his buttocks had ever experienced. He decided the clock must be specially regulated to tell lies about the time being wasted and the chair designed particularly to deter malingerers.

Matron appeared just as Albert decided he wasn't going to wait any longer for her permission and was about to set his size twelves on the sacred ground of her ward. Seeing her stern expression, he was glad he hadn't. She would have put the wind up the belligerent new Kaiser Wilhelm himself. Her uniform put scruffy police inspectors to shame, he thought, straightening his lapels and smoothing his hair. Her dark blue skirts whispered across the polished floor as she moved with the resolution of an ironclad battleship and just as intimidating. The sensible cloth was so heavily starched it could probably stand to attention on its own, and the knife-edged pleats might be used to shave off Inspector Abbeline's mutton-chop whiskers in no time – begging his pardon: newly Acting Superintendent Abberline. Her white apron, collar and cuffs were dazzling and her steel-grey hair was pulled back to the nape of her sturdy neck with such severity it made Albert wince. He had the feeling that if a single hair of her head dared stray, it did so at its peril and she would promptly take her scissors to it. The ensemble was topped off by a dainty, lace-edged cap but this was her badge of office, not a frivolous decoration.

'Inspector Sutton,' she said, 'This is not a convenient time. The consultant is due in a few minutes to make his rounds.' Her voice was authoritative as he'd expected but quite quiet. He was about to explain how police procedure was more important than a doctor's routine when she smiled and added: 'Perhaps you would like to take tea in my room while you wait, inspector? I prefer Darjeeling. Do you? There is seed cake too.'

Matron's room was also a surprise. A fire burned in the hearth and souvenirs of the Indian Subcontinent decorated the place: tasselled silk cushions and a bright rug. Sepia photographs of bejewelled maharajas and memsahibs wearing absurd bonnets, riding on elephants, adorned the walls. An oil painting of a broad-shouldered man in a pith helmet, rifle at his shoulder, standing over a huge dead tiger had pride of place above the mantle.

'That is my father,' she said, seeing his interest, 'General Sir Henry Bothwell. I was born in India; remained until my mother died of fever. Nursed her for a year or more. Decided I could put my knowledge to use here. England is cooler too.' She boiled a little kettle on a spirit stove and set out exquisite porcelain cups and saucers, chinking silver teaspoons. 'Of course, my mother always had servants to make tea. Have a chair. Will you take cake, inspector?'

'Yes, indeed, ma'am, if it's no trouble.'

She laughed; a sound quite at odds with her appearance. Albert realised that beneath her air of stark efficiency, Matron was a handsome woman.

He sat down in cushioned comfort in a high-backed armchair with a crocheted antimacassar and crossed his legs.

'Ma'am, indeed,' she said with a smile. 'Call me Victoria. Named for Her Majesty, of course – father's way of honouring the Queen, God bless her.'

'Albert,' said Albert, 'Not necessarily my father's way of honouring the late Prince Consort. Apparently, I was named after a horse that won him two shillings and thruppence in the Derby on the day I was born.' He didn't mention that the full name of the horse had been 'Lysander Albert', a moniker he preferred to forget.

'Well, are we not just the perfect pair?' Matron giggled like a girl. 'How do you take your tea, Albert?' She poured the amber liquid, added milk as required and then lifted the cover from a glass stand, revealing a golden seed cake at least five inches high. She cut a most generous slice that filled the dainty tea-plate and passed it to him.

Albert was quite disappointed when, just as he settled back to enjoy it, a nurse knocked on Matron's door to tell her the consultant was ready to begin his rounds.

'Forgive me, Albert. Duty calls, but do stay and enjoy your tea and cake.' With that, Matron left and he could hear her commanding her nurses like a sergeant-major. Or perhaps more like General Bothwell.

The tea was excellent and the seed cake unsurpassed. Albert was content to take his time; he was no longer in any hurry to interview the wretched Berkeley. What was the point, if the devil's mind was blank as a new sheet of blotting paper? Sadly, before he had quite finished his delightfully unexpected repast, a nurse came to inform him that the doctor's rounds were done and Matron said he could have a half hour with the patient. Quite ungentlemanly, he ended up stuffing the last of the cake into his mouth and gulping down the rest of his tea. Brushing crumbs from his waistcoat, he followed the nurse onto the ward, praying he wouldn't get an attack of the hiccoughs from bolting his food.

His first impression on seeing the scoundrel propped up by pillows was that he looked far too comfortable and well cared for. He deserved a cold, damp cell, awaiting the attention of the hangman; not a cosy bed and the kindly hands of pretty young nurses. Albert was also somewhat undecided as to the best approach in questioning him but, seeing other patients dozing quietly, one reading and two either gazing at nothing or deep in thought, a civil attitude seemed preferable so as not to disturb the ward.

'You may leave us, Constable Turner, thank you. Go stretch your legs,' Albert told the young policeman who had leapt from his chair at the foot of the bed to stand to attention.

'Thanking you, Inspector Sutton, sir.' Turner saluted and marched away, his firm footsteps sounding far too loud.

'Good morning, Mr Berkeley,' Albert said as he pulled the vacant chair closer to the bedside. He put his hat on the counterpane and took out his notebook and the pencil that Nell sharpened for him every morning.

'Is it?' Berkeley replied, barely speaking above a whisper.

'As you well know, I'm Inspector Sutton from Scotland Yard.' Albert sat down, discovering this chair was of the same design as the one in the waiting area and just as uncomfortable for his bony backside.

'Are you? Fetch me a glass of water, will you?'

'I'll ask a nurse to fetch it after you have answered my questions. Can you tell me your address, please?'

'Address? You mean my current abode? Well, here, obviously, wherever this place may be?' Berkeley waved his hand vaguely at the pale green walls.

'No. I require your home address.'

Berkeley shrugged and shook his head.

'I have not the least idea,' he said, as if this was the saddest news in the world. 'I was hoping someone would tell me for I fear I am quite lost otherwise.'

Albert realised this interview was not going well.

'Does Primrose Hill ring any bells?'

'It sounds a most pleasant place, but no, I don't believe I know it. A glass of water would be much appreciated. I seem to be always thirsty, lying here. A dry atmosphere, I expect.'

'Later.' Albert was losing patience and it showed. 'Then let us start with your name.'

'My name can be anything you wish since no particular one attracts me nor feels quite right. You may call me the Prince of Wales or the Archbishop of Canterbury, if you prefer? It is all the same to me, I'm sorry to say.'

'There are a few names I'd like to call you,' Albert growled under his breath. 'None of them suitable to be used with ladies present,' he added as a nurse wheeled a little trolley into the ward, rattling an assortment of brown glass medicine bottles. Each one was corked, labelled and, no doubt, contained the vilest concoctions known to man. That was how Albert viewed them, anyway. He couldn't even swallow liquorice flavoured cough linctus without gagging.

'I'm really very tired,' Berkeley murmured. 'Could we not do this some other time? I need to rest now. And will you bring me that glass of water, as I asked?'

'Here's your medicine, Mr Berkeley.' The nurse came over, an uncorked bottle and large spoon at the ready.

'Tell him I have to rest, will you? I'm not able to withstand his questioning. Tell him, nurse.' Berkeley was trying to sound pathetic and frail, but Albert didn't miss the spark of cunning in the felon's eye, brief as it was.

'I'm sorry, inspector, you'll have to leave. The patient must not be overtaxed: Matron's orders.' With that, the nurse proceeded to dose the patient with a thick brown liquid, elbowing Albert aside.

The sight and smell of the medication were sufficient to send the inspector hastening for the exit, eager for fresh air. Nonetheless, he was certain now, having glimpsed that momentary knowing look, that Berkeley's memory loss was just an act. The devil had no more forgotten his name than how to breathe.

~

That odious fellow, Sutton, left me in peace at last. Stupid as the rest of them, of course, yet I have the feeling he is the most dangerous. I might almost believe he suspects my ruse. But no. That would be to credit him with too great an intelligence.

I had much to accomplish this afternoon in order to set up my ingenious plans for tomorrow. My first intent was to establish whether the horseshoe magnet I procured yesterday was sufficient to the task required. If it was not, I must revise my *modus operandi* accordingly. An expedition to one of the communal lavatories was thus necessitated. There, I experimented with the magnet. The door was kept shut while the facility was in use by a bolt that also moved a coloured slider on the outside of the door from green, meaning 'vacant', to red, indicating 'engaged'. The door being constructed of solid oak, I was uncertain whether the magnet would have sufficient power to move the bolt through the thickness of the wood. As it happened, I should not have been concerned: applying the magnet to the slider on the outside also moved the bolt across on the inside of the door. Thus satisfied, I secreted the magnet high up, on top of the cistern, for future use and while standing upon the lavatory seat, I examined the length of chain that operated the flush. It was somewhat shorter than I should have liked, but I had a means in mind of remedying the deficit. At least it was of robust English manufacture with no soldered link in the length looking likely to fail if an undue weight was applied.

Now, all that was lacking was the appropriate victim: my lamb to the slaughter.

CHAPTER 27

Sunday, 11th November

MORNING DAWNED; the weather wet and blustery, as proclaimed by the view through the hospital window of the bare branches of a plane tree waving against a sullen sky and the intermittent splatter of rain against the glass. Excellent. Wind and rain meant the use of umbrellas and everyone's eyes downcast. Better yet, the minister was somewhat delayed in his arrival, so his interminable canting would likely last until luncheon. For this once, I feigned avid interest in the service, going to such length as to beg him to speak more slowly. I did not wish him to gabble his way through the proceedings in order to complete them at the normal time of one o'clock.

'I beg you, reverend sir,' I said, 'Give due reverence to Our Lord and speak decorously, that I may hear and ponder upon the words.'

He acknowledged my admonition with a nod and complied with my request. As a result, it was twenty-three minutes after the hour by the time he was done. He folded away his sermon notes and tucked them into the pocket of his shabby coat, closed his Bible and picked up his chaplain's black hat with its wide brim. When I asked him concerning the deeper meanings of some of the passages he had quoted, he became quite ardent in his discussions – not that I cared a jot for any of his theological nonsense – but my years of enforced attendance in chapel at Eton served me well in this situation, enabling me to pose questions that were requiring of detailed explanations. I knew the Book of Revelation was a subject that promoted a deal of controversy among churchmen, so I steered the conversation in that direction, certain he would have much to expound upon those particular texts. He did, and the clock stood at just seven minutes to the luncheon hour when I halted his lingual contortions by the simple means of asking him to assist me to the lavatory down the passage. I ignored the attempt at protest made by the spotty young constable who had seen me attend my ablutions unaided earlier. The minister, unwilling to lose his intelligent and attentive audience, continued his explanations as to determining the identity of the Whore of Babylon in chapter seventeen as I leaned heavily upon his arm all the way to the lavatory door. As if I had the slightest interest in such specious argument; his irrational self-deception.

As he pushed open the closest lavatory door, I made a pretence of overbalancing, dragging him into the cubicle with me. Upon the instant, I was a frail invalid no longer. I kicked the door shut even as my hands closed about his scrawny neck, my thumbs pressing down on his windpipe – my recent finger-strengthening exercises being employed at last. He quickly fell limp and I was able to bolt the door properly. I removed a short length from the bandages wound about my head, attached it to the handle of the lavatory chain and wound it securely around his throat. Such a pathetic specimen: he would be hardly worth recording in my journals except that he is the first man of the cloth that I have killed and the first I have hanged – by means of a lavatory chain. How droll, indeed. He succumbed to death so readily; it might be thought he was overeager to meet the God he spoke of with such enthusiasm. Even now, he will be learning the error of his beliefs, if the dead are capable of realisation.

Having re-pinned the remaining bindings to cover my wound, by which time the minister had ceased to twitch, I undressed him with the expertise of long practice. He was not the first victim I had stripped of their attire. I folded up the clothes neatly and set them and the shoes by the hand basin, hanging the hat on the hook provided for the towel. This last, I took with me. I left the Bible on the lavatory-paper dispenser. Having retrieved the horseshoe magnet and with the towel under my arm, I swiftly vacated the lavatory, closing the door behind me and using the magnet to slide the bolt across, so it appeared to be in use – as indeed it was: by a minister in all his naked glory. I secreted the towel-wrapped magnet in the laundry room next door, having determined by astute observation that the laundry was never attended to on a Sunday.

I then returned to my bed in time to be served a luncheon consisting of a slab of stringy meat, provenance unknown, lumpy mashed potato in an unappetising shade of grey and a watery, colourless mound of tasteless vegetable that may once have been a cabbage. While I ate this unpleasant repast, the young constable gave up his chair at the foot of the bed to Constable Michaelson. They exchanged a few pleasantries and Michaelson was smiling. I was hard put to contain my mirth, considering the afternoon's activities I had in mind to vex the wretch and ruin his prospects as a policeman forever. He sat down and unfolded the most recent copy of the *Police Gazette* – a favourite journal of mine, having spent many a pleasant hour laughing over the numerous cases of metropolitan incompetence and police ineptitude. I proposed to pass the hour of visiting time, doing my utmost to appear indifferent when I was, in fact, seething with impatience.

Shortly after the dreaded hour for visitation commenced, Matron appeared with a young woman whom she introduced to me as a 'lady-visitor' – an entirely unnecessary aberration invented to annoy patients who had neither family nor friends to distract them from more profitable mental exercise, as I soon discovered. Matron stated that she thought I would – and I quote: 'appreciate the kindness'. I did nothing of the sort, fearing this would ruin my plans and, of course, I had not the slightest interest in making petty conversation with such a foolish creature. The minutes ticked by as she attempted to engage my attention, prattling on about the weather, the latest news from Buckingham Palace and – something that did pique my interest – the discovery of the mutilated body of a prostitute, Mary Jane Kelly, in Whitechapel the day before.

'It's in all the newspapers. The police claim she must be Jack the Ripper's fifth victim,' the woman informed me with such unbecoming relish I almost thought I might take a liking to her. But, as ever, the police were wrong, as I knew very well.

At six minutes before four o'clock, she ceased her chatter, bade me 'Good afternoon' and wished me a speedy recovery. That was most certainly about to happen.

I instructed Constable Michaelson that I was in need of the lavatory. I had done this many times in the last few days, suggesting my bladder was failing me. At first, he had insisted on accompanying me, but that duty soon palled and he'd grown tired of the lengthy waits I had caused him, standing outside the lavatory door. Besides, my groans and moans from within had made unwholesome listening. Therefore, I left him to his reading as I retrieved the magnet from the laundry room, using it to unbolt the lavatory door. Inside, I took a moment to savour my earlier handiwork, the pallid corpse, dangling by the neck, his tongue swollen and protruding, his eyes open but unseeing. Divesting myself of the detestable borrowed pyjamas – or whatever they call them – I swiftly dressed in his clerical attire. The cassock was a little short and the shoes rather tight but no matter. Removing the bandage from my head, I replaced it with the chaplain's hat to hide my injury and partially shaven hair. I tied the pyjamas into as small a bundle as possible, using the remaining length of bandage like a length of parcel string to bind them and stuffed them behind the cistern. I knew the corpse would soon be discovered, but there was no need to leave evidence of my identity to be found so easily.

Bible in hand, I left the lavatory, bolting the door by means of the magnet just as Matron rang her absurd little bell to indicate that visiting time was ended. I joined the throng of departing relatives, keeping my head low as I descended the stairs. A woman bumped my elbow and apologised, calling me 'Reverend', so I touched my hat courteously and blessed her in the name of God. Such hypocrisy; I could not help but smile. And then I went out, through the hospital doors, into the beautiful English drizzle and freedom. However, it did not escape my notice that one man was entering the hospital against the tide of those leaving. It was Inspector Sutton, no less, and I touched my hat to him and he to me. No reason for ill-manners between a man of the cloth and the city's finest police officer.

CHAPTER 28

ALBERT LOATHED hospitals at any time but to have to visit again on a Sunday afternoon was too much to ask when he should have had his feet up in the parlour, reading the newspaper, enjoying Nell's company with his belly full of her best attempt at roast mutton and Yorkshire pudding. A gourmet dish it would never be – her culinary skills were limited at best – but it was a comfortably hearty meal on such a cold and miserable day.

Foolishly, yesterday, with the entire force rocked and sent chasing their tails by another Whitechapel murder, Albert had informed *Those Upstairs* and Abberline that he was just about certain Berkeley had not lost his memory or, if he had, it was now returned. As the new Superintendent, grasping at straws and determined to impress, Abberline wouldn't waste a day – even a Sunday – before questioning the fellow further and had sent Albert a telegram to that effect, ordering him to interrogate the miscreant forthwith. Hence the inspector's arrival at St Thomas's. Needless to say, he was not in the most pleasant frame of mind. A miserable drizzly grey fog rising off the Thames, clinging to his coat and fingering his face with its icy touch, did nothing to cheer him either. On the steps before the doors of the hospital, a departing cleric or vicar or whatever he was touched the brim of his hat to Albert, obliging him to return the polite gesture, despite feeling far from courteous. There was no cause for churlishness with others, he told himself, not when his anger was against his newly-promoted superior and no one else. Apart from the unknown perpetrator of the latest killing in the East End who had upset the entire city.

At least he was now out of the damp and gloomy November twilight and the recollection that Matron might be there on the third floor to greet him had him bounding up six flights of stairs, two at a time. He was rewarded: Matron Bothwell – Victoria – was there, in the waiting area, looking stern and efficient as ever, until she saw him. Then the hint of a smile twitched at the corners of her mouth and was it just the glow of the freshly-trimmed oil lamps that reflected in her eyes? Or were they twinkling with the pleasure of his return? Albert liked to think it was the latter case. She certainly illuminated the dull winter afternoon and improved his mood no end.

'Would you care for a cup of Darjeeling, inspector? I usually take tea after visiting time, while my nurses are settling the patients prior to supper.'

If only all police matters might be conducted in such a genteel manner, Albert thought as he sipped his tea and nibbled on dainty fingers of Scottish shortbread. Victoria was telling him about the hair-raising incident in her childhood in India, when she had found a hooded cobra under her bed and her mother sent for the local snake-charmer to entice it out.

'So you see, Albert, far from always being intent upon a career in nursing, my first ambition was to be a snake-charmer, complete with turban and flute. What of you? Did you always want to be a policeman?'

'Indeed not, dear lady. Like a thousand other lads, I always longed to drive a locomotive. Still do, if I'm honest. The idea of making that whistle blow as we hurtle into the darkness of a tunnel and the magic of daylight rushing towards us at the far end; the heat of the firebox, the gush of steam, the squeal of brakes and clattering over the points. I love the thought of it, even though on a wind-blasted footplate at the dead of night, covered in soot and half-frozen, I might change my mind.' Why was he telling Victoria his private thoughts? Nell had never asked him about his hopes and dreams.

'How very wise and practical of you to consider such drawbacks. Do help yourself to more shortbread.' She offered him the plate and he took another melting, buttery delicacy. 'And do you find policing more accommodating?'

Albert swallowed and pulled a wry face.

'London's backstreets can be just as cold and dark on a winter's night. Just as many soot smuts and freezing winds. At least on the footplate I'd always have company and the warmth of the firebox.'

'Your job is a lonely one?'

'Sometimes. Especially when I was a lowly constable on the beat. Thank goodness someone invented the whistle. Like that on a steam loco, it's an excellent means of calling attention. And that's probably as close as I shall ever get to my childhood ambition – blowing a policeman's whistle.'

'Do you still carry one, now that you're an inspector?'

'Yes. It's always in my pocket. You never know when it might come in useful.' He fished in his inside pocket and took out the slim, silver object, lately restored to him upon his reinstatement, along with his warrant card and keys to his desk and the filing cupboard.

'May I?' Victoria held out her hand.

Somewhat surprised, Albert gave her the whistle.

182

With a girlish grin, she put it to her lips and blew a little experimental 'peep'.

'I wonder why we both find such instruments fascinating? I should love to deafen everyone with a truly shrill blast but better not. Hospital rules, you see.' She laughed and put the whistle down beside her teacup.

At that instant, there came a splintering crash followed by just such a shrill blast from outside: a woman's scream.

Albert was out of his chair at such a rate the spoons rattled in the saucers. Matron was half a step behind him.

One of the lavatory doors was swinging back with a crash for the second time. Constable Michaelson was panting from the effort of having put his shoulder to the door, fearing a patient must be *in extremis* beyond the bolt.

'He went t' the necessary, sir. Never came back. Thought he'd passed out in there, sir. Never thought...' Michaelson stepped back so Albert could see the crime scene.

The young nurse was still hysterical and Matron summoned one of her colleagues to take her aside and give her a cup of tea with plenty of sugar.

For a moment, Matron and Inspector surveyed the scene side by side.

'Your jurisdiction takes precedence in this case, Inspector Sutton, I believe. I'll leave you to it. Anything you need, just ask.'

'A spare bedsheet and a patient's trolley, please, Matron. Come along, Michaelson, let's get the poor fellow down. Who is he? Do we know?'

'I think it's the minister who does the Sunday service,' Michaelson said.

'Can't be. I saw him leaving as I came in a half hour ago. Touched his hat to me, as if he knew me but...' Realisation dawned. 'Where's that devil you were guarding?'

'I thought it was 'im what was locked in 'ere, sir. Oh, Gawd. He's gone, ain't he?'

Albert was torn between his duty to the victim and the need to pursue the culprit. After a moment's hesitation, he decided the hospital couldn't function properly with a body hanging in the lavatory and, besides, trying to chase down a felon in the fog was likely to be hopeless anyway, so the few minutes it took to secure the corpse and cover it decently would make little difference.

Informing his superiors was quite another matter. Michaelson was going to be in trouble over this. It wouldn't do his own tarnished reputation much good either – happily taking tea while the felon walked away right under his nose and with sufficient temerity to bid him 'Good day' as he departed the premises.

With the deceased laid out on a trolley and shrouded in a sheet for the sake of decency, Albert had the constable wheel it out of sight, into the laundry room, to await the hospital orderlies to take it down to the mortuary in the basement. Albert sighed. There was one thing to be said for a murder committed inside the walls of St Thomas's: it was most convenient for the carrying out of the necessary *post-mortem*. He watched as two nurses began cleaning the lavatory cubicle, scrupulously scrubbing every corner.

'Sir, there's this,' said one, finding a bundle of clothing, tied up with a length of bandage, jammed behind the pipework of the lavatory cistern.

'They're 'is pyjamas,' Michaelson said, shaking his head and looking forlorn.

'Indeed. Well, set them safely aside, constable. Look sharp now. We have ourselves a felon to apprehend.' Albert was all businesslike of a sudden. There was a job to be done and no time for Michaelson to mope and wallow in self-pity for his shortcomings. 'The safety of Londoners is in our hands,' he added.

'Yes, sir. S'pose we best go searchin' then? But where to start, eh?'

'Good question, constable. I believe I saw someone dressed as a cleric when I arrived. If I remember correctly, he was turning to the left at the foot of the entrance steps. That was my impression, at least. I fear I paid him little attention at the time. Even then, that might have been a ruse to mislead me. He's as crafty as a whole circus full of monkeys, that one. We must make enquiries as we go. People might remember a clerical gentleman.'

'What if 'e takes them clothes off, sir?'

'Then the devil will be naked as Adam and even more memorable.'

''Less 'e takes someone else's again.'

'Unfortunately, Michaelson, that is a definite possibility we must take into account.'

'Might even be dressed in women's stuff, like 'e did before.'

'I haven't forgotten. Come along. Have you got your weapon to hand?'

'Yes, sir. Never leave 'ome without me trusty truncheon but what about you, Mr Sutton? You got a pistol or sommat? You might need it.'

'No. I was hardly expecting to require such a thing, not for a hospital visit on a Sunday afternoon. Just my wits and my whistle. They'll have to do, such as they are.'

CHAPTER 29

ONCE OUTSIDE the hospital, I saw a clerical gentleman clad much like myself, standing with a queue of common people beneath one of the gas lamps on Westminster Bridge. Like a flock of stupid sheep, they waited in the damp, foggy night for a public omnibus. Such a means of travel was abhorrent to me, though I had made use of such vehicles in the past when a particular disguise merited it, but in this case, it might serve my purpose perfectly. I realised, though, that I was at the grave disadvantage of having no money upon my person. The foolish minister, whose attire I now wore, appeared to have forgotten to avail himself of the requisite finances to enable me to pay the fare or to hire a hackney carriage. Either that or his wallet had been dropped during the brief scuffle that ensued before I succeeded in winding the bandage and lavatory chain about his neck. I smiled at the remembrance of that moment, observing the wretch as death claimed him. He hardly struggled against it which was a pity indeed. I appreciate a good fight.

I spoke to my fellow churchman, greeting him courteously before telling him a masterful tale of woe.

'Good evening, sir,' I said, offering him my hand. 'I see

we are of a like mind on such a dismal night, though I had not intended it so. Oh, begging your pardon: my name is Oscar Merriweather – the Reverend Doctor Merriweather, Rector at St Margaret's.' I did not say at which church of St Margaret, knowing there were so many places of worship thus dedicated.

'Walter Vernon, vicar of St Botolph's in Aldgate.' He shook my hand.

'Ah! So you are also heading towards Whitechapel. What a coincidence. Perhaps we might travel together?' Whitechapel was as suitable a destination as any and I knew the area intimately. It was the perfect place of concealment since, no doubt, that confounded nuisance Sutton would be attempting to search me out soon enough. His endeavours would prove fruitless, of course, in that vipers' nest of prostitution and debauchery.

'I should like that,' he said. 'Your company will be most welcome on the journey. The Number 5 omnibus to Whitechapel should arrive shortly. It's a shame it's dark and foggy, otherwise we could see the new bridge they're building by the Tower. It's already raised to quite an impressive height. Have you seen it?'

'No. I have little reason to travel that way, St Margaret's being in the opposite direction, but this is a small mission of mercy and one that has gone awry, I fear.'

'How so?'

'An elderly parishioner lies on his deathbed – consumption, sadly. He wants to see his daughter one last time but has been unable to discover her whereabouts. Now, at this eleventh hour, I have learned that she abides in Whitechapel. Her profession is utterly repugnant to me, as you can imagine, but I promised the poor fellow I would bring her to him, if at all possible. But now I must admit to having an ulterior motive in introducing myself to you, my friend. You see, I have no coin to pay my fare on the omnibus. My own fault entirely. I gave sixpence to a poor soul I saw begging outside Lambeth Palace, two pence to a fellow beneath the railway arches and a penny to a barefoot urchin by the steps down to the Thames. Like a fool, I have left myself with only a note for one pound sterling remittance and I realise there will be little likelihood of change enough to be had on an omnibus.' I waved a piece of crumpled paper I had found in a pocket of my purloined coat. 'So I was wondering if you might spare a few coins of lesser denomination?'

'My dear fellow, of course. Such kindly acts should not be to your detriment,' he said, taking out a leather purse. 'Here. Will five shillings be enough? And here are some pennies and a couple of threepenny pieces for the fares. You'll be wanting to come home again after and if the girl comes with you, she'll probably expect you to pay for her too.' He pressed a pile of loose coins into my hand.

'Bless you, sir. I am enormously in your debt,' I told him, slipping the money into my pocket. 'Tell me your address so I might repay you.'

'You can always find me at St Botolph's but why not simply put that amount into your church alms box? It will save you an extra journey.'

'I am so grateful and shall certainly be glad to do that.' Of course, I had no intention of doing such a thing as wasting money on the so-called 'needy'. They would only waste it on drinking and gambling.

The omnibus arrived – late – and my new-found friend and I were jammed inside with a crowd of stinking humanity such that one hardly dare draw breath for fear of some noxious contagion being inhaled. The Reverend Vernon looked at home in the press of foul bodies, but I became quite dizzy and nauseated by the stench. Perhaps my concussion was not yet fully healed for I am not usually thus afflicted. I determined then never to travel by means of such fearful public transport again. A first-class compartment on a train is one thing; a third class seat on a crowded omnibus is hell upon earth.

'Where are the first class seats?' I asked my companion as we were crushed together on a slatted wooden bench.

'No such thing on an omnibus,' he said, bracing himself against me as the horses took us around a tight corner at quite a pace. 'We're all equal here. Have you never travelled this way before?'

'Never. And shall not again. I fear the crowd and the lurching and jolting are making me feel quite unwell.'

'Not much farther to Tower Hill now. Why don't you get off there with me? You can come to the vicarage and have a brandy restorative, if you will? Set you up for your visit to Whitechapel on such a horrid night. I don't envy you, Rector Merriweather, and commend your stout heart for venturing there at all, especially at such a late hour and after what happened to that unfortunate soul, Mary Kelly. She was one of my parishioners, you know. Still, I doubt the misguided fellow they call the Ripper has much interest in our kind.' He took out his watch and held it to the meagre light of a smoky oil lamp that was all the illumination in the wretched vehicle. 'My, my. It's a quarter after six already. You could join me for supper. My housekeeper cooks a fine bacon pudding.'

The mention of food almost caused me to vomit. I tasted bile at the back of my throat.

'A tempting offer,' I managed to say, 'But my mission... urgent.'

'Of course. A pity though. I should have liked to discuss my idea for next week's sermon with a fellow cleric. I had in mind a new approach to Matthew chapter 5, verse 8, you know? "Blessed are the pure in heart..." My dear fellow, you are looking quite peaky. Shall I ask the conductor to have the driver stop?'

'No.' I breathed deeply, though the foetid air hardly aided my constitution. 'I am recovering now. A momentary thing was all...' Despite my words, when the vile contraption came to a halt by Aldgate and my companion disembarked, I did likewise. Having my feet on firm ground and able to breathe again, though it is difficult to comprehend, the sulphurous smoke and acidic fog smelled fresh as country airs after being confined in that ghastly omnibus and I felt much improved in moments.

'Brandy?' my companion offered once more, but I declined, insisting my journey to Whitechapel must be accomplished on foot now and, therefore, with greater urgency.

'Who can say how long before my ailing parishioner may be called to God?' I said. 'The physician believed a matter of hours; no more. I thank you again for the loan, my friend. May the Lord be with you.'

'And also with you,' he responded, as befitted his calling and mine, supposedly. He tipped his hat and went on his way, disappearing into the fog. I might have killed him, had I so wished but having observed the death of one cleric today, where was the novelty in slaying another, unless some unique twist of circumstance presented itself? Since it did not, I determined there would be more original opportunities in this part of London and my attire added further possible nuances to their execution. I anticipated the celebration of my regained freedom with relish but with whom should I share such pleasures? My choice of victim was now a matter chance for them; a delightful prospect for me.

CHAPTER 30

AS LUCK would have it, as Albert and Constable Michaelson made enquiries outside St Thomas's hospital, a tattered old beggar, sheltering in the angle between the marble steps and the wall of the building, had seen not one but two men in clerical garb.

'The first gave us tuppence for a cuppa – as if that helps on a Sunday when the public houses, tearooms and cafés is all shut,' the beggar complained, scratching at his neck beneath a matted beard. 'Other one looked away, like I was invisible, miserable bugger. Churchmen? Huh! Tight-fisted the lot of 'em.'

'Where did they go, these churchmen?' Albert asked, deliberately chinking coins in his pocket.

'How would I know? I mind me own business, don't I?'

'Might you have minded someone else's, if there was a florin in it for you?'

'Maybe? For two florins, I might have.'

'Four bob! That's an outrage!' Constable Michaelson said, grabbing the vagrant's ragged coat. 'You tell the inspector what you saw or else...'

'No, no,' Albert said, speaking softly and gesturing for the constable to unhand the fellow, 'Good information is worth a reward of some kind. Half a crown, if you answer my question.'

'What question?

Albert saw Michaelson was ready to beat the information out of the stubborn old man, bunching his fists. He moved to stand between them.

'Where did the clerical gentlemen go? In particular, the one who gave you nothing.' Albert couldn't imagine their escaped felon giving a beggar anything except perhaps a knife in the gizzard or a rope around his throat.

The fellow shrugged his shoulders beneath his grimy coat.

'Three shillings, then. Not a bent farthing more,' Albert said. He too was losing patience.

'Both got on the Whitechapel omnibus, didn't they? The Number 5. That's all I know, 'cept the one what ignored us was wearing someone else's garb. Not a vicar at all, I reckon.'

'How could you tell?' Albert was interested now.

'Trousers and the gown thing he wore –'

'Cassock?'

'Mm, the cassock was too short to be his own and the shoes pinched him. I could tell by the way he minced along, he must be curling his toes up inside them shoes. I've seen enough of how folks look in too small clothes and borrowed boots. Reckon he stoled 'em. That's what I think. Now, do I get me money?'

Albert took out a handful of change and turned, so the coins were illuminated by the gaslight on the edge of the kerb. He sorted through them and chose two shillings and two sixpences.

'It's a shame you can't tell me where the one in the tight shoes intended to get off the omnibus.'

'No, but I heard 'em talking and the other one – him what gave us tuppence – said he was the vicar at St Bitoff's by Aldgate.'

'You mean St Botolph's?'

'That's what I said.'

Albert gave the coins, plus another sixpence, into the mittened hand that shot out to receive them.

'We're much obliged to you, Mr er...'

'Frank. Just Frank.'

Albert nodded and smiled.

'Get yourself a bed for the night now, Frank,' he said. 'I don't want you adding to my workload tomorrow as another frozen body to be identified. Good night. Come along, constable, we've got an omnibus to catch.'

It was a long, cold wait. Omnibuses were few on a Sunday, but Albert was cheered to see Frank get to his feet and stumble off in the direction of a cheap hostel for the indigent in Addington Street. At least he would be warm and safe for the night. As for himself and Michaelson, matters were less certain.

At last, four horses came around the corner from Waterloo Railway Terminus, drawing the Number 5 omnibus, clattering and swaying behind them, lanterns dimmed by the thin grey wisps of fog wafting off the river. The omnibus had few passengers at this hour and the policemen could choose their seats on the benches.

'Two to Aldgate, please,' Albert said to the conductor who took the sixpence he offered, punched two cardboard tickets in the machine that hung around his neck and returned them with the change.

'What's the Met coming to when their men can't afford a hackney?' the conductor said with a laugh. 'Economising so they can afford that fine new building, are they? A police chase on a 'bus, is it?'

'In a way, yes,' Albert said. 'We are pursuing a line of enquiry. Can you tell us who would have been the conductor on this route at sometime around half past four this afternoon? We're interested in two clerical gentlemen who got on by St Thomas's about that time.'

'That would be me. Shift runs from midday to nine in the evening on a Sunday, worse luck, so me and Stanley, the driver...' he waved towards the front of the vehicle, 'We're still on duty.'

'Do you recall seeing the gentlemen in question?'

'As a matter of fact I do. I was pretty wary of one of them, you see.'

'Why? What made you suspicious of him?'

'Well, see, I know some people don't take to travelling on an omnibus. They say it's the swaying and these inward facing seats they don't care for. Now the Reverend Vernon often travels to Aldgate and back with us. He visits his sister every Sunday for dinner along in Royal Street. But I never saw his mate before and I don't think he ever rode an omnibus before either. Even asked where the first class seats were, daft so-and-so. By the time we were at Charing Cross, he was green as grass and I was worried he'd puke up everywhere and guess who'd have to clean up the 'bus afterwards? Me, of course. So I was watching him and keeping my fingers crossed. I was thankful when Reverend Vernon hauled him off at Aldgate, I can tell you.'

'That's most helpful. Thank you. Where are we now?' Albert peered out through the mud-splattered window but, since it was dark outside, the window only reflected the interior of the omnibus and the occasional glimmer of the gaslights was all that he could see of the streets passing by.

'Fleet Street. Soon be in the city.'

'Long route,' Michaelson muttered, grimacing. He didn't much like omnibuses either.

'Don't worry. Won't take long at this time of night. No commercial drays on a Sunday dawdling along, blocking the roads, and too early for theatre-goers in their fancy carriages. Not that there are many of them once we're beyond Covent

Garden. We'll have a straight run along Cornhill and Leadenhall to Aldgate. Then we're into Commercial Road where this route terminates. Then it's back to Waterloo and we're done for today: the last 'bus. Were you thinking of coming back with us? If you were, you'll only have about twenty minutes or so at Aldgate before we return, though Stan and me could probably take our time, turning round. Give you half an hour, if you want? Doubt there'll be any passengers, anyway. Longer than that, they'll dock our pay for not keeping to the timetable.'

At Ludgate, a solitary man alighted and at the stop by Mansion House a young couple got on but, as the conductor predicted, there were few passengers.

'Thank you for the suggestion', Albert said after considering the possibilities. 'But don't wait on our account. Wouldn't want you to lose any wages. We don't know how long this business may take, do we constable?' He nudged Michaelson who was slumped on the bench beside him, looking miserable as a wet washday, as Nell would say. The thought of her suddenly reminded him that she would have been expecting him home for supper by six o'clock and, checking his pocket watch, it was now almost eight. Nell would be frantic with worry. He ought to have got off at Mansion House where there was a police station next door and sent a message by telephone to Scotland Yard. Then they could have got someone to go to Summerlea Villas and tell her he would be late home but it was passed the time for that now.

All the passengers, bar one, got off at Aldgate and the sole remaining traveller looked to be a hefty docker or seaman, to judge by the tattoos on the backs of his shovel-sized hands, the sort who lived in the rookeries of Whitechapel. No other respectable citizens were likely to stray there on a foggy Sunday night when the East End was at its most villainous. Unfortunately, Albert worried, that was likely to be just the place where they would have to go to find their absconded felon. But firstly, they would call at St Botolph's vicarage, to make certain the Reverend Vernon had not fallen victim to the devil.

CHAPTER 31

The East End of London

I WALKED southwards towards the river, down Mansell Street, feeling the chill cut through the clothes I wore. They were of such inferior quality; I may have been garbed in butter-muslin for all the warmth they rendered. I had in mind to turn along East Smithfield until it became The Highway. Of old, it was the infamous Ratcliffe Highway, haunt of prostitutes, pimps, opium-dealers and gin-distillers and the change of name had singularly failed to alter its nature one jot. Even the likes of scavengers and street-sweepers did not venture there. However, since the observation of Sunday licensing laws did not exist in such a place and I was desperate for a warm hearth and a brandy, I would go where few would dare. Besides, I knew these vile rookeries well enough – once the haunt of Jack the Ripper until I had settled the matter, saving the Metropolitan Police a great deal of trouble, if they did but realise it.

Yet now, in my need, I had a stroke of good fortune. By St Katharine's, a new road was obviously under construction, and since navvies are ever inclined to drink away their wages, a public house had been lately opened close at hand. *The Bridge*, as the sign informed me it was called, likewise had little time for petty laws and the place was open and doing considerable trade. Even from outside, the noise was quite deafening after the near-silence insisted upon on the hospital ward where I had latterly been ensconced. Someone was pounding out a selection of music hall ditties on an untuned pianoforte. My connoisseur's ear detected that the F sharp key above middle C was flatter than a well-pounded veal cutlet and the ebony key for G sharp either wasn't working or else was missing entirely. Nonetheless, even such a cacophony of discord could not divert me from the necessity of warming myself, so I went in through the portals of the public house.

At sight of my clerical hat, there was a brief lull in the raucous racket and the customers made way for me. I realised most of them were likely navvies and therefore Irish Catholics by birth. Hence their respect for a man of the cloth.

'Welcome, father, and won't ye be having yer first glass on the house?' the landlord said by way of greeting. He was as Irish as a peat bog by his speech.

'Indeed, my son, that will do me roight well,' I said, adopting a southern Irish accent like his own. My ability to mimic foreign accents was superlative as ever.

'Whiskey or me own potcheen? What'll ye be having, father?'

'Potcheen,' I said. Never a Scotch or Irish whiskey drinker – brandy being my preference – I determined his own distillation would serve me better and suit the role I played. I admit I may have been somewhat in error in making that choice. A lethal concoction of sulphurous acid, iron filings, broken glass and gunpowder – for such it seemed to be – near blew one's brains out and scoured the tongue raw.

'Ay, 'tis a goodly brew o' fire-water that,' the landlord said as a customer thumped me on the back so I might draw an inward breath and tears ran down my cheeks. 'But the fellas here need it, working on that new bridge out there. Yer seen it, father? Quoite a soight it is, I be telling yer.'

The customers all agreed with him and began relating their tales to me, their exploits in the construction of two colossal towers that were now rising either side of the river. Apparently, there was great rivalry between these men working on the north bank and those across the Thames in Southwark, working on the south tower. They swore the north tower was at least a month further advanced than the south, almost an entire level of scaffolding higher as they were now raising the third tier. In Southwark, the second tier was not yet secured, they informed me.

As I grew warmer, my intellect was piqued by this new Tower Bridge construction. The vicar – Vernon – had told me it was well worth seeing and the more I heard of it, the more it intrigued me. Its possibilities as a venue for death were quite enticing but what of my specimen? No one here would be suitable. No doubt, they could all climb like monkeys and the scaffolding would hold no terrors for them. Besides, I had no weapon, and though a broken beer bottle might serve to intimidate, it was too barbaric and working class for me to make use of except as a means of self-defence at the last resort. However, a working class means of murder, perpetrated by a clerical gentleman would be an interesting addition to my collection.

And how to persuade anyone to ascend to such precarious heights in the dark? The answer to this was self-evident, at least. Anger. Anger made people reckless and prone to errors of judgement. I could not entice a specimen to climb with me, but I certainly had the capacity to so enrage my chosen subject for experiment that they would cast aside all caution and pursue me, wherever I should go, of their own volition. Such was the plan now developing in my mind but, as already iterated, none of the customers at *The Bridge* would serve my purpose for fear they would be more nimble and agile and thus render me at a grave disadvantage. The recent blow to my head and my subsequent time in the hospital had been to the detriment of my fine physique, softening muscles and reducing my strength. Thus, unlike the one I should select as my next specimen for study, I must exercise care upon mounting the scaffolding in the darkness.

The pretence of acting the cleric was beginning to pall, being so alien to my nature, so once warmed through, I blessed the drunken denizens of the public house and disappeared into the night. The first stage of my plan required a decent set of clothes that would rebuff the chill air while not hampering my movements as the wretched cassock did, such that climbing anything more challenging than a flight of stairs in this attire would be foolhardy in the extreme.

Considering the new experiment I had in mind, an excursion into Whitechapel would take me away from Tower Bridge, so I retraced my steps back towards Aldgate. It happened that I was standing by the sign that indicated the alighting and embarkation point for those hateful omnibuses when the vehicle itself came in view, firstly as a ghostly apparition materialising from the fog and then as a thing of substance, preceded by the jangle of harness and the clop of hooves on the wet cobbles. I raised my hand as I had seen others do to command it to halt. The team of horses steamed in the cold night air, stamping and blowing. I approached the open platform at the back where the conductor stood, waiting to assist me.

'Never thought to see you travelling with us again, vicar,' he said. 'You didn't enjoy your last ride with – .'

I grabbed his coat and in an instant flung him from the platform into the roadway with all the strength I was able to summon. I then pulled the communicating cord that rang a bell behind the driver, indicating that he could move off. As the omnibus departed, I leapt from the platform to discover what Fate had sent me. I recognised the conductor as the same fellow I had observed in this capacity earlier and he was dressed suitably to stand, exposed to all weathers on his platform for hours together. He wore a knitted scarf tucked inside his uniform great coat and I pulled free the two ends, tightening them about his throat before he had fully mastered his befuddled wits after his hard landing. Unable to cry out, he struggled gamely for a few minutes, long enough that my hands and arms were aching with the effort of strangling him, but then it was done. I dragged him to a nearby alley and proceeded to unclothe him – more by touch than sight in so dark a place – then to disrobe myself and put on his still-warm attire in haste. The undergarments and uniform were a far better fit than the clergyman's vestments and the boots were more accommodating than his thin-soled shoes.

I discarded the naked remains where they lay. The lackey had been merely incidental to my plan; his death of no consequence nor interest but to supply more suitable clothing. He was of no account otherwise.

CHAPTER 32

The East End

THE REVEREND Walter Vernon opened the vicarage door to the inspector's knock. He was wearing carpet slippers trodden down at the back and a tattered shawl around his shoulders when he came to the door.

'How may I help you, sirs?' he asked when Albert showed him his warrant card. 'Why don't you come in, out of the cold? Would you like a cup of tea? Or something stronger, perhaps, on such a chilly night?' Vernon led them into a pokey little parlour, a meagre coal fire glimmered in the grate and a single oil lamp cast a smoky yellow light over a side table. Reading glasses and thick volume – the Bible, maybe – lay open on the table, an ageing armchair drawn up close. 'Tea?' he repeated.

Constable Michaelson was about to say 'yes, please', but Albert shook his head. Glancing at the open book, he was surprised to see the name Charles Dickens heading one page and the title *A Tale of Two Cities* heading the other.

Not holy scripture after all.

'No, we won't trouble you, vicar. We just stopped by to make certain you were safe.'

'Safe? And why would I be otherwise?'

Albert didn't want to scare the old gentleman unnecessarily by telling him he had travelled on an omnibus and held a conversation with a serial killer.

'Just a report we had of some troublemakers in the vicinity of St Botolph's. But since all is well, we will bid you goodnight and advise you to lock and bolt all your doors and windows tonight.'

'I will do that, inspector. Thank you for the warning. I can see that the police are doing their utmost to keep us all safe. Thank you again.' The vicar showed them out and shut the door. The reassuring sound of a stout bolt being pushed into its hasp had Albert nodding approval.

'I could have done with the cuppa he offered,' Michaelson muttered.

'Cold, constable?'

'I'll say. I can't feel my ruddy toes in these police-regulation boots. Same every winter. I'll have chilblains by weeks-end, if not frostbite.'

'We have a villain to catch. A bit of pavement-pounding will soon warm you up. Look lively, constable.'

'Yes, sir, Mr Sutton.' Michaelson sounded anything but lively. He'd had in mind a cosy game of dominoes at his cousin's house off Whitehall, then a sing-song around the piano after. Not trudging the wet, foggy streets of the East End, searching for some murderous bugger. That was no way to spend a Sunday evening.

Albert too would have much preferred to be at home with Nell and the cat, or at Scotland Yard even. Anywhere but here. They crossed the cobbled street. There were neither pedestrians nor traffic, all sensible people being at home by their fireside, like the Reverend Vernon.

'What now, Mr Sutton? How do we find him?'

Albert was wondering the same thing when a glimpse of something starkly white caught his attention in an alleyway. Nothing in this part of London ever remained so clean and bright for long and had it been any other colour, it wouldn't have shown up in the unlit gloom. Even before he investigated it, he had a grim premonition of what it was. Sure enough, the devil had been at work yet again.

'He's not far off, constable; the body's still warm, poor fellow. And we know him.'

'Do we?'

'It's the conductor on the Number 5 omnibus. The fellow we spoke to earlier. At least we now know what the wretch is wearing. Run to Mansion House Police Station, Constable Michaelson. Tell them about this and bring reinforcements and lanterns... and pistols. We may need them.'

Michaelson was gone, disappearing into the murky night, down Tower Hill. Albert turned his attention to the corpse. He laid it straight, but it seemed indecent to leave it naked. There was a pile of discarded clothes beside the body and he used the clerical cassock to cover the dead man's face and body. It was the best he could do for the unfortunate conductor.

'Well, Sutton, so you found my most recent handiwork. Not a thing of beauty, I'm afraid: no planning nor finesse involved on this occasion.'

Albert leapt to his feet, turning to see a shadowy shape against a background of faint light from a gas lamp in the street at the far end of the alleyway. A few stray tendrils of fog curled around the figure, making it seem unreal, a thing conjured from the ether. But Albert knew who it was.

'Berkeley, you unholy scoundrel. You'll pay for this.' Albert felt the rage within him turn to an icy calm. He knew the time of reckoning for this monster was at hand:

no court case, no judge and jury. Just the two of them. He walked towards Berkeley who backed away before turning and breaking into a trot. He wasn't fleeing, Albert realised breaking into a run to apprehend him.

Yet, somehow, he never quite caught up. Each time Albert came close to grabbing Berkeley, the devil would put on a sudden burst of speed, so the chase continued. The fog was thinning and the moon showed its pale face, casting an eerie light as they ran. The road surface beneath his feet was new and led towards the river. Up ahead, strange shapes were silhouetted against the moonlight, looming high above the water. Berkeley was running towards the structure that would become the newest bridge across the Thames: the marvellous feat of engineering to be known as Tower Bridge. It made no sense, Albert thought. Berkeley was going to be trapped at the river's edge. Why would he come this way? Surely he must realise that.

Albert was panting, his breath making white clouds in the cold air. A stitch in his side didn't help, but he couldn't stop now. When Berkeley ran out of road, he had to be there, so he went on playing cat and mouse, chasing after the figure in the conductor's uniform.

Just as the river came in sight, its foetid waters looking deceptively beautiful, sparkling beneath the stars that were appearing as the fog dispersed, Albert lost sight of Berkeley as he ran into the building site. For a few moments, he disappeared among the clutter of construction equipment and steel girders. Then Albert spotted him, climbing a ladder that was tied to the lattice-work of scaffolding. Already, he was up to the first level. Albert was in two minds. Should he wait at the bottom for Michaelson and the reinforcements? It might take time for them to track him down here but at least he had his trusty whistle. He reached into his pocket where he always kept it. It wasn't there. A moment's panic: he always had it. Where was it?

Then he remembered Matron asking if she might blow it and, in all the confusion, when Michaelson had broken into the lavatory and discovered the body of the minister, he must have forgotten to pick it up. So now he couldn't summon help or attract attention. Still, the felon wasn't going anywhere soon.

Or he could follow Berkeley up the scaffolding? What purpose would that serve? He couldn't say but realised that elaborate scaffold-work reached out from the tower above, stretching towards a matching structure on the far bank, a tangled, interlacing web of planks and poles, outlined against the moon. Did Berkeley think he could escape that way, one hundred and fifty feet above the Thames? The gap was too wide for any man of sense to attempt to cross. But Berkeley was a madman and maybe he believed he could confound and embarrass Albert yet again with some impossible means of eluding him? With his patience at an end and a determination to avoid any further dent in his fragile reputation, Albert knew without a doubt what he would do: he too was going to climb Tower Bridge.

CHAPTER 33

Tower Bridge

WASN'T THAT just typical of the wretched devil? Albert could see Berkeley's figure one hundred feet up, bathed in moonlight, climbing the scaffolding, nimble as a damned squirrel. He had no chance of keeping up. His boots kept slipping and his hands were numb with cold. Having realised knitted gloves gave little grip, he'd taken them off. The scaffold planks were so slick with moisture, it was like skating on the ice of the Serpentine in mid-winter and Albert would admit he wasn't much of a skater. Twice on the first level, he skidded, barely managing to keep his balance. Scaling the long ladders that bowed under his weight to reach the second level was terrifying indeed. He'd always believed he had a good head for heights. Now he wasn't so sure.

Albert had to pause on the second level to catch his breath, but Berkeley was nowhere to be seen and must already be on the third. In the quiet of the night, the inspector heard the Thames sucking and slurping like a rabid dog around the bridge foundations below: a reminder of what fate awaited him if he fell. The muffled clangs of ships' bells wafted on the rising breeze from the numerous vessels rocking at their moorings in the Pool of London.

There was also the sound of a steam tug, chugging along, the hissing and wallow of its wake churning the water as it passed downriver, towing a chain of barges from Blackfriars, taking the street-sweepings of mud and horse dung away from the city. Indeed, now it was closer, the stench on the wind proved its identity. This would be but one of dozens of barges, going about their smelly nocturnal business every night, removing the excrement of London to the marshes of Essex.

That Berkeley had climbed higher was confirmed as a bombardment of steel rivets hailed down, clattering on the scaffolding as a sack-load was emptied on him from above. They pounded on Albert's head and shoulders, denting his new Homburg and making him wince in pain when they hit him. Insane laughter added to the sound of the turgid waters lapping at the stanchions. Again, Albert reached for his whistle, but the pocket remained empty and he cursed his earlier carelessness.

The moon rode high now and the fog cleared as the wind got up. Skeletal fingers of cloud clawed across the moon's bright orb. Albert shivered and pulled his knitted scarf to cover his ears. The rain of rivets ended so he hurried to the next ladder. Such haste was a mistake. His feet were in the air of a sudden and he came down hard, flat on his back at the very edge of the planks. He scrabbled for a hold, grasping at the slimy surface, frantic not to slip into the blackness below. Every bone was jarred and the breath knocked out of him as he pulled himself back from the brink. Taunting laughter echoed again into the night.

Determined to ignore his hurts and, worst of all, his humiliation, Albert got up, taking more care. As he began to climb the ladder up to the third stage, the wind caught his hat and it was gone in an instant, before he could grab it, tumbling away, disappearing forever into the river of darkness below. At the top of the ladder, he peered over the lip of the wooden decking. There was no sign of Berkeley. Fearing he might be attacked at any moment, he inched up, hauling himself onto the scaffold planks, looking all around. Still no sign. Then he saw him, standing at the far end, where the upper causeway was being built out, across the river, to meet its companion half that jutted out from the south tower. The wind gusted strongly at this height and Albert wondered at the wisdom of being so exposed as Berkeley was now, standing close to the edge of the causeway. He had been right: the scoundrel must intend to escape by reaching the other tower.

'Come on, Sutton,' Berkeley shouted, his tone scornful. 'What are you afraid of? I am quite unarmed.'

'I have no fear of you, you murdering bastard,' Albert yelled back. The wind tugged at his coat, making him unsteady again and seemed to snatch his words away. He was unsure Berkeley would hear them.

'Heights distress you, do they, inspector?'

'Certainly not.'

'Then come along. We have matters to discuss, do we not?'

'I have nothing to say to you.'

'Then why did you come? Why follow me here?'

'To arrest you.'

Berkeley laughed, rocking on his feet.

'I shall enjoy observing you as you attempt to do so. Come. Put your restraints on my wrists. If you dare? If you can?' He held out his hands, ready for the inspector's handcuffs.

Albert knew it was a trick. Taking this felonious fiend would not be that easy. He moved forward slowly, cautiously, never taking his eyes off Berkeley. The moonlight glinted off the brass buttons of the conductor's uniform great coat. Albert could now judge that there was no way of crossing to the south tower from here. The gap must be at least sixty feet wide or more. Even Berkeley wasn't mad enough to attempt that leap, so it seemed likely he would seize any chance to dart past Albert to make his escape as they came closer. Either that or he would try to shove the inspector over the edge. A midnight swim in the river was not part of Albert's plan. Not that he had much of a plan. This had been a terrible mistake. Trembling, shivering in the wind, Albert did his utmost to put on a brave face, but his resolve had dwindled, fading away like the fog. Perhaps he should simply climb back down the ladder, untie and remove it and leave Berkeley up here to freeze to death. Now *that* was a plan. His mind made up, he turned to walk back to the ladder.

That was when a locomotive hit him. That's how it felt. Berkeley fell on him at full speed from behind, knocking him down, face first, onto the slick wooden boards.

'You won't escape me so easily as that,' Berkeley hissed in his ear. 'Did you not realise, inspector? *You* are my next experiment. You may drown immediately, or you may swim in that typhoid-riddled river, to die a week hence of the ghastly contagion. You have the choice after I commit your body to the deep. Either way, you *will* die. Farewell, Inspector Sutton. Rest assured, I shall send my fulsome condolences to your pretty wife.'

It took all Albert's strength to heave his assailant off his back, losing a handful of hair in the wretch's grip as he did so. He grabbed Berkeley's coat as, grappling and rolling together, they inched once more towards the edge of the decking. Albert punched his opponent wherever he could: in the face, the chest or belly, but most of his blows seemed to land harmlessly. Unlike Berkeley who knew exactly how to inflict damage. A fist to the jaw made Albert's sight explode with fireworks and a knee in his kidneys made him cry out and forced him to swallow down bile. This fight wasn't going his way.

Berkeley scrabbled halfway to his feet. Albert did the same, moving away from the edge, but they were both staggering like drunkards. Now wasn't the time for the Marquis of Queensbury's rules, not when it was a matter of life or death. Albert had tackled enough violent criminals in the past to know how to fight dirty. The polite policeman was now a ferocious opponent. Berkeley grabbed Albert's coat, threatening again to pull him over the side. Albert reached out and his fingers found an ear. He ripped at it and Berkeley squealed, recoiling sufficiently that Albert had a precious moment of time to aim his next blow straight between the eyes, only to slip and lose his balance, so the punch caught Berkeley's shoulder instead.

Berkeley flew at him and both men went down again, clawing for purchase to keep from falling over the edge. This time Albert's questing fingers went for the eyes but his opponent turned aside and he missed but found the nose instead, twisting it as sharply as he could. The sound of crunching cartilage and a piercing cry told of the damage done, but then Berkeley rammed his shoulder into Albert's chest, knocking him back. Albert's groping hand found a scaffold pole to cling on to, but it was loose and might be his weapon. Yet it was too long and unwieldy and Berkeley grabbed the other end. A fearful tug-o'-war followed until Berkeley wrenched it sideways and Albert had to release his grip to avoid tumbling into the darkness below. Berkeley threw the pole away, and it fell, clanging and thumping, as he leapt forward again, seizing hold of Albert's scarf – the one Nell had knitted. Just like the conductor's neck apparel, it was perfect for the purpose of strangulation.

Albert fought and squirmed but Berkeley was sitting

on his thighs and the scarf was tightening around his throat. He needed air. His strength was draining away. His lungs were bursting; his eyes bulging. In a last effort, he brought up his knees and lunged forward, smashing his forehead into Berkley's already broken nose. The villain's hands were clutching at his ruined face and, for a moment, Albert was able to gasp a breath as the scarf loosened. He rolled on his side, away from the edge, so he thought. He was wrong. Berkeley was lurching, slipping and grabbing at him and suddenly Albert realised there was nothing beneath his left leg. It was hanging in space. Berkeley screamed, clinging to one end of the scarf. Albert tried to pull the other end from around his neck, but then the plank began to tilt, tipping until they both were falling into the void. This was the end.

Their rapid descent ceased in a bone-wrenching jolt. Albert dangled from the scaffolding, suspended by his scarf wrapped around his chest. Looking down, he could see Berkeley holding on grimly to the other end. The scarf had snagged on a scaffold pole that extended out over the river. Now they hung balanced at either end of Nell's ever-stretching scarf. Albert gripped the pole above with frozen hands, trying to pull himself back onto the wet planks but Berkeley's weight was dragging him down, pulling at his feeble grip. He couldn't hold on; his fingers were slipping.

Then, with the last ounce of his strength, Albert managed to swing his foot up and hooked it over the pole. With one hand, he loosened the scarf, succeeding in slipping the last loop off, over his head ,so the end of it came free. Relieved, he let it go. The scarf fell. And Berkeley fell too with a terrible scream.

Albert hung from the pole, lungs heaving, gasping for air. He was expecting to hear a splash. Instead, there came a sound more like a squelch and a gloop. He looked down to see the running lights of another steam tug, trailing a line of more barges full of excrement, passing under the bridge on its journey downriver. In the third barge, illuminated by the pitiless moonlight, the spread-eagled form of Nathaniel Grosvenor-Berkeley was gradually sinking, face down into the foul cargo. Consumed by shit, what a dire end, Albert thought. It was the kind of death you wouldn't wish on your worst enemy. But, then again, it was a novel method of extermination the Death Collector could add to his list.

EPILOGUE

Monday, 19th November

Albert and Nell were sipping tea at Mrs Mumbles' tearoom. Albert was still finding it difficult to swallow anything, his neck raw, both inside and out, from being almost strangled – and saved – by the scarf Nell had knitted for him. As the new man in charge at Scotland Yard, Superintendent Abberline had insisted that Albert was taken straight to St Thomas's Hospital after his encounter with Berkeley on top of Tower Bridge. Albert had done his utmost to protest but, unable to speak because of his swollen throat, nobody took any notice. However, his deep dislike of hospitals was swiftly overcome when he was put to bed in a private room on the third floor and Matron Bothwell attended to his needs in person. No hospital food for her precious patient. Instead, because of his inflamed throat, it was a menu of various soups of the smoothest, most delectable kinds, all made by her own capable hands and spoonfed to him by her good self. No other nurse could be trusted to care for her dear inspector. He had now recovered for the most part but facing Nell's concrete pastry crusts was still out of the question. Hence, a visit to the tearoom where Kitty Mumbles' Viennese sponge cake, assisted by a sip of tea, slipped down his throat quite easily.

'I'm sorry I lost the scarf, Nell,' Albert croaked. The doctor had said his larynx was badly bruised and it would be a week or so longer before his voice was back to normal.

'But it saved you from falling, so it served a purpose.' Nell spread more strawberry jam on her cheese and onion scone and took a bite. 'Besides,' she said after swallowing it, 'I know you hated the colours.'

'I never did.'

'Yes, you did, but I shall knit you another in Metropolitan Police blue. Then you never need be ashamed to wear it.'

'I never was.'

'I'm so pleased he's gone, Albert, so relieved.' Nell poured more tea for them both.

'Indeed and it was just in time, too, saving lives for certain. On the day we first caught him –'

'You mean when Blackstock caught him.'

'Yes, well, that very evening he was planning to shoot a butler at Brown's in St James: Maurice Culpepper. It was all noted down in his journals. Thank goodness he didn't get the opportunity. And he had already decided he was going to push some, as yet, unnamed person onto the railway track at Euston Station in front of the 12.45 from Birmingham New Street: he had it all worked out. I think we may have saved many lives, Nell.'

'At least London is a safer place now; a better place to bring up our baby.'

'I suppose it will be if we ever find out who killed Mary Kelly in Whitechapel the other week,' Albert said, licking his finger and dabbing up the last crumbs of sponge cake on his plate.

'That was Jack the Ripper, surely?'

'Mm, maybe...' Albert didn't want to dwell on that mystery.

'How's Constable Michaelson bearing up?'

'Abberline gave him a severe reprimand for letting Berkeley dupe him like that and escape, so I'm told, but at least he's only been suspended for three weeks without pay, rather than sacked, so there is a glimmer of hope. I believe the sterling effort it must have taken him to get me down from Tower Bridge has caused *Those Upstairs* to be a little more lenient. Mind you, two more murders as a result of the escape won't look well on Michaelson's record of service. Whatever befalls though, I probably owe the lad my life. Any longer up on the scaffolding and I should have frozen to death if it wasn't for him finding me, so I intend to see him right regarding money while he goes unpaid.' Albert cleared his throat carefully: too much talking hurt, so he poured more tea and drank it down.

'I'll be glad if we can help him out. He's such a nice young man.'

Albert gave Nell a look that said more than words.

'Don't be silly, Albert. I didn't mean it that way. It's just that he's always polite and he likes Blackstock too, which must be in any man's favour. Perhaps we could invite him for supper one evening? Only to spare his purse while he has no wages.'

Albert nodded but had no intention of inflicting his wife's culinary efforts on any unsuspecting soul, particularly not a fellow to whom he owed his life.

'We could all go to *Bennett's*,' he said. 'You could invite your friend Betsy Briars along: we'll make a foursome, so Michaelson doesn't feel too awkward.'

'That's a splendid idea!' Nell clapped her hands in delight. 'He and Betsy will make a fine couple. What's his Christian name?'

'Now, now, Nell!' Albert spluttered and coughed as his last bite of Viennese sponge went down the wrong way. 'Don't you go match-making.'

'Why not? We're well suited: a policeman and a flower-girl, so why not them? Betsy is such a kind-hearted, hard-working girl. And pretty too. And the constable... What did you say his name was?'

'I didn't.'

'Oh come, Albert. If he's going to sup with us, I can't call him 'constable' all the time, now can I?'

'I think his service record says 'V. Michaelson', so maybe it's Victor or Vincent? I don't know.'

'You work with him, yet you don't know his name?'

'It's just the way it is, Nell.'

A screeching of chalk on a blackboard attracted their attention. Mrs Mumbles was adding to the day's menu.

'Oh, look, I really fancy some of that, Albert. May I order a portion of kidney fricassee? Will you have some as well?'

'No. Certainly not. I never want to see, let alone eat, another kidney in my life. Not after...' He couldn't bring himself to finish the sentence. 'And if you have any sympathy for me, Nell, you won't eat such a thing in my presence, either... not ever. Come, let's catch the omnibus to Jermyn Street: I shall be needing yet another new hat before I return to work. You can choose it for me, sweetheart.'

THE END

READING GROUP QUESTIONS

1. This novella was written tongue-in-cheek as a Victorian 'melodrama', intended to be over-the-top gory, spooky and a bit of a joke – a sort of pastiche on Edgar Allen Poe's *The Murders in the Rue Morgue*. Do you think it works?

2. Rather like many Victorian novelists, I wrote *The Death Collector* as a serial. Dickens did this with most of his books, publishing them as part-works in magazines and always ending each episode with a cliff-hanger. Did the chapter endings make you want to read on and, if not, how do you think this might have been better achieved?

3. Many of the murders featured are true crimes, some of which were never solved. Others are my invention. Do you feel this mixing of fact and fiction adds to the story or does it confuse the reader?

4. How realistic did you find the setting of Victorian London? How might the story have changed if it took place in a rural setting or even in *fin de siècle* Paris?

5. The character of Nathanial Grosvenor-Berkeley is supposed to be exaggerated. How did you feel about him? Did you find him scary or ridiculous?

READING GROUP QUESTIONS

6. I had the idea for a detective marrying a flower-girl after watching *My Fair Lady*. Did you find Albert and Nell's relationship convincing or was it too much of a fairytale?

7. Blackstock the cat is vital to the story as it stands but what differences would it make and would the story still work if this farcical element was left out?

8. Which of the minor characters most caught your interest and why? Could that character have been further developed and, if so, how?

9. In your opinion, what were the underlying themes of the story – if any?

10. Personal reaction – what did you enjoy or particularly dislike about *The Death Collector* and would you suggest it to a friend?

As an author, I welcome comments and thoughts from everyone who reads my books. It would be lovely to hear from you, so please head over to my website and get in touch with me. I hope that at some time we'll be able to chat about history, writing and ... murders!

www.ToniMount.com

MORE FROM TONI MOUNT...

In the amazing "Sebastian Foxley Medieval Murder Mystery" series, you'll get to meet Seb, an illuminator who works near to St Paul's Cathedral. In the narrow stinking streets of medieval London you'll discover murder around every corner...

The Colour of Poison
The Colour of Gold (novella)
The Colour of Cold Blood
The Colour of Betrayal (novella)
The Colour of Murder
The Colour of Death (novella)
COMING SOON: The Colour of Lies

"5.0 out of 5 stars - love the portrayal of life in the middle ages... brutal, with small bits of kindness"

"5.0 out of 5 stars - another brilliant read... you feel like you are back in medieval times"

AVAILABLE NOW FROM YOUR FAVOURITE BOOKSHOP

Historical Fiction

The Sebastian Foxley Murder Mysteries - **Toni Mount**
The Death Collector - **Toni Mount**
Falling Pomegranate Seeds - **Wendy J. Dunn**
Struck With the Dart of Love - **Sandra Vasoli**
Truth Endures - **Sandra Vasoli**
Cor Rotto - **Adrienne Dillard**
The Raven's Widow - **Adrienne Dillard**
The Claimant - **Simon Anderson**

Non Fiction History

Anne Boleyn's Letter from the Tower - **Sandra Vasoli**
Queenship in England - **Conor Byrne**
Katherine Howard - **Conor Byrne**
The Turbulent Crown - **Roland Hui**
Jasper Tudor - **Debra Bayani**
Tudor Places of Great Britain - **Claire Ridgway**
Illustrated Kings and Queens of England - **Claire Ridgway**
A History of the English Monarchy - **Gareth Russell**
The Fall of Anne Boleyn - **Claire Ridgway**
George Boleyn: Tudor Poet, Courtier & Diplomat - **Ridgway & Cherry**
The Anne Boleyn Collection - **Claire Ridgway**
The Anne Boleyn Collection II - **Claire Ridgway**
Two Gentleman Poets at the Court of Henry VIII - **Edmond Bapst**

PLEASE LEAVE A REVIEW

If you enjoyed this book, *please* leave a review at the book seller where you purchased it. There is no better way to thank the author and it really does make a huge difference!
Thank you in advance.

Printed in September 2021
by Rotomail Italia S.p.A., Vignate (MI) - Italy